Natalia moved slowly ~~~, feeling as if someone had ~~~~~ her in the stomach. She couldn't believe it. As if things weren't bad enough already!

Her new coach was a disaster. Her new school was a disaster. She didn't fit in at home, either. Veronica still kept crazy hours, and Mrs. Carsen didn't seem to know what was going on. Several times Natalia woke up to the sound of teenagers giggling outside her window. Veronica didn't seem to care that she was disturbing Natalia's sleep.

As for Tori, Natalia couldn't quite figure her out. Some days she was friendly, but other times she seemed to resent Natalia just for being around. And she was very competitive on the ice.

And now this! A tryout, when Natalia's skating was at its all-time worst!

She could just imagine the tryout. Everyone would laugh at her skating, just as they'd been laughing at her ever since she got here.

What would happen if she failed the tryout? She could be kicked out of Silver Blades before she'd even gotten started! What would her father say? And how would she ever face Tori and her friends again? She'd be totally humiliated!

It's the end of my dream, Natalia thought. But she wasn't even sure it was her dream anymore.

NATALIA COMES TO AMERICA

Melissa Lowell

Created by Parachute Press, Inc.

A SKYLARK BOOK

NEW YORK • TORONTO • LONDON • SYDNEY • AUCKLAND

With special thanks to Darlene Parent and
Sky Rink Skating School, New York City

RL 5.2, 009–012

NATALIA COMES TO AMERICA

A Skylark Book / March 1997

1

Natalia Cherkas flew across the ice. She moved smoothly into a camel spin. The rink blurred as Natalia whirled around and around. She smiled. It feels so good to be skating again! she thought.

A week before, Natalia and her father left their home in Moscow, Russia. A whole week since she'd been on the ice! Natalia could hardly believe it. She hadn't been *off* the ice that long since she first started skating, ten years ago.

But Natalia's father needed her help settling into his new job as ambassador to the United States. Moving from Moscow to Washington, D.C., was a big change for both of them. When they arrived in Washington, Natalia spent most of her time trying to make Mr. Cherkas's hotel room feel like home. She ordered his favorite foods from nearby restaurants and placed photographs of herself and her sister, Jelena, around the room.

The rest of the time, her father sent her on tours of the famous buildings in Washington. And at night Natalia watched TV to polish up her English. Then, finally, her father was settled and ready to bring her here, to the ice rink in Seneca Hills, Pennsylvania.

This is it, Natalia told herself. This is where the famous Silver Blades is based. Silver Blades was a well-known skating club. It was an honor to be chosen to skate here. Natalia's father had pulled a few strings to get Natalia into the club. Luckily she had a top reputation back in Russia. And she had had excellent tapes of her skating to mail to the coaches in Seneca Hills.

Natalia smoothed her brown hair and gazed around the rink. She was in love with the place already. The arena held two Olympic-sized skating rinks—one for figure skating, one for hockey. There were huge locker rooms and separate rooms for weight training and ballet lessons. All perfect, absolutely perfect! she thought with pleasure.

Natalia moved into a fancy footwork sequence and then let herself glide across the ice. She checked the big clock on the wall. In a few minutes, she and her father would meet her new family, the people Natalia would live with in America.

Natalia knew the family had a daughter, Tori Carsen. Tori was also a member of Silver Blades. She was supposed to be an excellent singles skater, maybe the best in the club.

Secretly Natalia hoped she and Tori would become friends. She already missed having someone she could talk to, the way she talked to her older sister, Jelena, back home. No matter what, I've got to make a good impression on the Carsens, Natalia told herself.

Voices floated across the rink, interrupting Natalia's thoughts. Two girls stepped onto the ice and began warming up. One girl was very pretty, with blue eyes and curly blond hair. She looked about fourteen, the same age as Natalia.

The girl wore a pale lavender skating dress with tiny silver sequins at the neckline and across the flesh-colored inset at the back. More sequins decorated the close-fitting sleeves. The skirt was divided into petal shapes, and at the end of each petal was a tiny, teardrop-shaped crystal.

Natalia gaped. The dress was fancier than most of the dresses Natalia wore in competitions! Why would the girl wear it for an ordinary practice session? Natalia wondered. She thought for a moment. Of course! The girl probably had an important competition coming up, and she was wearing the dress now to make sure it moved well through her program.

"Hey, watch this," the younger girl cried, zipping past the blonde.

The younger girl was a petite brunet about eleven or twelve years old. She was dressed in black leggings and an oversized pink sweatshirt—just like Natalia's outfit of white leggings and a long blue sweater. Natalia did some crossovers and three-turns, but at the same time, she watched the girls with open curiosity.

They glanced at her once, then looked away. The brunet easily launched into a triple Lutz–double toe loop combination. Natalia's mouth dropped open. The young girl was incredibly good!

The blonde glided past Natalia, rolling her eyes and looking bored. "Big deal, Amber," she called. "I've seen you do that combo a million times before."

"But did you see how high I got this time? On *both* jumps," Amber answered. "Kathy said my height is amazing."

The blonde shrugged, unimpressed. "So what? I can get just as high."

"Oh, yeah? Let's see," Amber challenged.

Natalia stopped skating and watched the others with interest. The blond girl skated around the rink, building up speed. Then she jumped. Her triple Lutz was good—nearly as high as Amber's—but she didn't get enough height on the toe loop. She completed only one and a half revolutions, and her landing was shaky.

"Oh, right, really good," Amber teased.

The blonde scowled. "I was just warming up. That didn't count," she said.

The blonde circled the rink again. This time she performed an inside Mohawk back crossover, then took off into a flawless triple Lutz–double toe loop. She landed squarely on her right foot and swung her arms open wide—then threw back her head with a triumphant smile.

She turned toward Amber. "Bet you can't do *that*," she said.

This time Natalia was impressed. The combination was beautiful, graceful, and solid. Both of these girls were as good as Natalia, and she was the best at her rink back in Moscow. Well, maybe the best. Her sister, Jelena, was as good as she was, Natalia admitted.

Natalia wondered if Amber and her friend were members of Silver Blades. What would it be like to skate with them every day? They were obviously competitive, but that was okay. That would challenge Natalia to skate her best.

Amber whirled into action again, right in front of Natalia. Her skating was somehow changed. Natalia stared—then realized with a start that Amber was imitating the blonde!

Every move Amber made was a perfect copy of the older girl's manner. The tilt of her head, the way she held her arms . . . everything. Natalia bit back a smile and glanced at the blonde. From the look on her face, she didn't like the imitation act one bit.

Amber finished with an inside Mohawk back crossover, then took off into a triple Lutz–double toe loop. She, too, landed squarely on her right foot, then threw her arms open wide and her head back with a very theatrical smile, blinking her eyes rapidly.

Natalia giggled.

"What's so funny?" the blonde demanded.

"Oops!" Natalia giggled again and covered her mouth with her hand. "Uh, nothing is funny," she said.

The blonde stuck her nose up in the air. "Let's see you do something simple. Like, a double axel," she dared. "If you have one, that is."

Natalia looked the blonde squarely in the eye. "Of course I have one," she said.

The double axel wasn't usually a difficult jump for Natalia. But lately she was having a lot of trouble with it. Her timing was off, and she just couldn't seem to get it back.

But she would never admit that to the blonde. Not after that kind of a challenge. I can do it, she told herself, squaring her shoulders. It's an easy jump!

Natalia glided into backward crossovers to build up speed for the jump. Then she turned and launched herself into the air. As soon as her blades left the ice, she knew she didn't have the height she needed. She completed two revolutions before she was down again. She tried hard to hang on to her landing, but she two-footed it, anyway. Ulp! she thought.

When she turned around, the blonde was standing by the boards with her arms crossed over her chest, smirking. "Nice landing," the girl said in a voice dripping with sarcasm.

Natalia felt her cheeks burn with embarrassment. She shrugged, trying not to let her feelings show. "I *can* do it," she insisted. "And much harder jumps, too. But no one is perfect all the time."

"Well, I—" The blond girl stopped talking suddenly. She turned at the sound of approaching footsteps. Natalia turned also. She saw a tall, distinguished man with dark hair and serious brown eyes approaching them.

"Natalia!" he called. "Come here, please."

"Papa!" Natalia called back. She skated across the ice toward her father. He was walking with an elegantly dressed woman at his side. The woman was blond, and her features seemed somehow familiar.

"Natalia, this is Mrs. Carsen," her father said. "The woman you'll be staying with."

"Mrs. Carsen!" Natalia rushed forward, her brown eyes twinkling in excitement.

"Welcome to America, Natalia," Mrs. Carsen greeted her. "We're all so excited about your visit! I'm sure it will be a wonderful experience for all of us."

Natalia smiled. She was impressed with how beautifully Mrs. Carsen was dressed. And with her wonderful manners.

"Thank you, Mrs. Carsen," Natalia answered politely.

"Oh, no, please call me Corinne," Mrs. Carsen told her.

"Okay, Corinne," Natalia said.

Mrs. Carsen nodded to the blond girl who had skated up to Natalia. "I'd introduce you to my daughter, but I see you've already met. Tori, come say hello to Natalia and Mr. Cherkas," Mrs. Carsen said.

Natalia gaped at Mrs. Carsen. No wonder she seemed familiar! She looked just like her daughter. She turned to face the blonde. "*You* are Tori Carsen?" she asked.

"The one and only," Tori answered. She turned and skated back to the center of the ice.

"Come on, Amber," Tori called. "Let's practice some more."

Natalia almost groaned aloud. So much for making a good first impression, she thought. What have I gotten myself into?

2

Natalia flung open her suitcase. It rested on one of the comfortable twin beds in the guest room. Tori sat cross-legged and watched from the large upholstered chair by the window.

"What I don't get is why you decided to come here," Tori said. "Why not just stay in Washington with your dad?"

Natalia glanced at her. Tori had seemed friendly enough on the ride back from the rink, but Natalia hadn't forgotten the way Tori had challenged her—and laughed at her—on the ice.

"Well, Papa couldn't find a rink that he thought was very good in Washington. Not for a skater at my level," Natalia said.

"That's important, all right," Tori agreed.

"And he also thought I would be happier staying

with a family," Natalia continued. "Papa works all the time. He knows someone who knows your mother, and they knew all about Silver Blades. So Papa arranged this for me. He talked to a Mrs. Bowen about it, I think."

"Sure. She's the president of Silver Blades," Tori told her. "She's great."

"Yes. She arranged for me to train with Coach Trapp. She said he is very good. Do you know him?" Natalia asked eagerly.

Tori laughed. "Oh, yeah, I know him," she said. "He's my coach, too. You can call him Dan, you know. Everybody does."

"Okay," Natalia said. "But, what is he like? Is he strict? Marina Voda, my coach in Russia, she was strict about *everything*."

Tori laughed again. "Dan? Strict? Hardly. Our other coach, Kathy Bart, is much tougher. Dan is a good coach, I guess," she said. "But he takes a little getting used to. Or a lot of getting used to."

"Why?" Natalia asked.

"He's different. You'll see," Tori replied.

Natalia frowned. "But, what do you mean? How is he different?"

Tori shrugged. "It's kind of hard to explain. He's just different, that's all."

Why wouldn't Tori answer her question? Natalia wondered.

Tori stood up and peered into Natalia's suitcase. She lifted a stack of sweaters and tops.

"Here," Tori said, "let me help you unpack." She fingered the sweater on top, then lifted it up and checked out the one underneath. She looked up at Natalia, obviously surprised. "Oh. Your clothes are so ordinary," she blurted out.

Natalia stared at her. She was so rude! "What do you mean?" she asked. "What is wrong with my clothes?"

"There's nothing wrong with them," Tori said, not even noticing that Natalia was insulted. "It's just that Veronica came here from Europe, and her clothes are *incredible*."

"Veronica—she is your stepfather's daughter?" Natalia asked. "And this is her room?"

"Right," Tori said. "It used to be our guest room, until Veronica showed up. Anyway, it's a lot bigger than my room, so we put you in here with her." Tori shook her head. "I never thought Veronica would stay this long, but now it looks like she's here for good. Lucky us," she added in her sarcastic tone of voice.

"But that's great, that you have a sister now," Natalia said. "My sister and I are very close, like best friends."

"How come she stayed in Russia?" Tori asked.

"Well, I am the one who always dreamed of skating in the United States," Natalia explained. "It was my choice to come here. Jelena wanted to stay in Moscow." Natalia sighed. "I already miss her so much."

"You wouldn't miss Veronica, believe me," Tori said.

Natalia stared at her for a moment, then picked up another pile of clothes.

"Veronica's mother's tailor in Paris made all her clothes, just for Veronica," Tori told her. "They're the latest styles, and absolutely gorgeous," she gushed.

Natalia glanced at the sweaters Tori was still holding. They had come from the best stores in Moscow. Natalia couldn't help feeling offended.

She took the sweaters out of Tori's hands. "Where should I put these?" she asked politely.

Tori opened a dresser drawer. "I think Veronica made room for your stuff in here," she said. She pulled out another drawer. "Yeah. This dresser's empty, Nat. Put them in here."

Natalia frowned. She had never liked being called "Nat." But she decided to say nothing about it, for now.

Tori walked to the closet. She pushed open the door and peered inside.

"It looks like there's a little room in here, too," Tori said. "Sort of." She gave Veronica's clothes a shove. The closet was so packed, the clothes hardly moved at all.

"That's all right. I have enough room in the dresser," Natalia said. She placed her sweaters in the drawer. She pulled several pairs of jeans out of her suitcase and stuck them in another drawer.

"I really thought your clothes would be more like Veronica's, since you're both from Europe and all," Tori went on. She lifted one of Natalia's skating dresses off the bed and found a space to hang it up in the closet.

"You were wearing a beautiful dress at the rink today," Natalia complimented Tori.

"Thanks." Tori shrugged. "My mom makes all my skating outfits. She's a clothing designer, you know," she added proudly.

"I know," Natalia said. She waited for Tori to pay her a compliment also. That was the polite thing to do in Russia.

"Well, it's too bad you have to room with Veronica," Tori said instead. She made an exaggerated sad face. "Poor Nat. It's not a great arrangement. But you'll survive, I guess."

Natalia felt herself stiffen again at the name "Nat." Again she wanted to protest, but she stopped herself. After all, she and Tori had just met. And she was Tori's guest.

Natalia's father had taught her always to be polite, and there was no sense starting an argument over a name. Still, Natalia couldn't help wondering if living with Tori's family was really such a good idea.

Tori plopped down on the edge of the bed. "So, what's it like having a father who's a diplomat?" she asked. "Do you travel all over the world with him?"

"Oh, no," Natalia replied. "Not at all. Papa does

travel a lot, but Jelena and I always stay home with Grandmother. Papa wants us to keep up with our studies. And our skating," Natalia added. "Going with him on his trips would make that too difficult."

"Oh. So I guess only your mother goes with him," Tori said.

"No," Natalia said quietly. "My mother died when I was only three. I don't even remember her."

"She *died*?" Tori looked shocked. "My mom didn't tell me that. What happened to her?"

"She was hit by a car, crossing a busy street in Moscow," Natalia said, lifting another stack of clothing out of the suitcase. "She was only thirty. The driver was speeding. They never even caught him. The doctors said she died instantly."

"That's terrible," Tori said. She shivered slightly. "I can't imagine what that would be like," she added. "My mom and I are so close. She was the only family I had . . . until she married Roger, anyway."

Natalia nodded. Her father had told her that Tori's mother recently married Roger Arnold, who owned several department stores. Tori's mother kept the last name Carsen for business purposes.

"Your mother and father—they are divorced?" Natalia asked.

"Yeah," Tori said. "They got divorced a long time ago, when I was only six months old. I met my father for the first time last year. I still don't know him very well. But now, of course, there's Roger."

"Your stepfather," Natalia said.

Tori laughed. "That still sounds funny to me! They've only been married two months. I'm not quite used to it yet."

"I can imagine." Natalia smiled and Tori smiled back.

Mrs. Carsen and Natalia's father appeared in the doorway. "Hey, girls," Mrs. Carsen said. "How's it going in here? Are you getting Natalia settled?"

"Uh-huh," Tori answered.

"It looks like you two are chatting like old friends already," Mr. Cherkas commented. "That's wonderful." He glanced at his watch. "Natalia, I have to leave now. I've got a lot of work waiting for me back in Washington, I'm afraid."

"You are not afraid at all," Natalia said affectionately. She walked over to her father and put her arm through his. "You love all that hard work," she teased.

"It's true. I do," he said. He wrapped one arm around Natalia's waist and gave her a little squeeze. "Just like you love to work at your skating."

Natalia laughed.

"That's good to hear," Mrs. Carsen said briskly. "Because we keep to a pretty tight schedule here. Skating practice every day, except Sunday. Five forty-five in the morning and two-thirty in the afternoon. I don't know what you're used to, Natalia," she went on, "but at Silver Blades—"

"Oh, Natalia is used to practicing for many hours

every day," Mr. Cherkas said. "I'm sure she'll have no problem adjusting."

"Especially not with that wonderful rink," Natalia agreed. "It's just beautiful, Mrs. Carsen."

"It is," Mrs. Carsen agreed. "But remember, call me Corinne."

"Oh, that's right! I forgot," Natalia said. "Corinne."

Mr. Cherkas smiled. "I really must go. Will you walk out to the limousine with me?"

"Of course," Natalia said.

Her father took her arm. Natalia kept a smile on her face all the way downstairs and out to the front door.

"Well, you're almost on your own," Mr. Cherkas told her.

"I know, Papa. You will call, though, will you not?" Natalia asked.

"Of course," her father answered.

Natalia was used to saying good-bye to her father. Still, he had never left her behind in a strange new house, with new people, in a new country before.

Natalia felt tears sting the back of her eyes. She blinked them away and smiled even harder at her father.

He bent and kissed her lightly on the forehead. "Good-bye, Natasha," he said, using their familiar nickname.

"Don't forget to call me soon, Papa," Natalia said.

"I won't," Mr. Cherkas promised.

Mr. Cherkas hurried quickly down the path to the waiting limousine. Natalia waved until the car disappeared around the corner. Her hand dropped to her side. She felt a pang of homesickness.

"Well," Mrs. Carsen said, "I guess this is it, Natalia. The official beginning of your new life in America." She checked the gold watch on her slender wrist. "I'm so sorry Veronica wasn't here to meet you and your father. I know she was dying to, but she has a big test next week. She's studying at her friend Betsy's house, and I'm afraid she'll be getting back late tonight."

"Yeah, right, *studying*," Natalia heard Tori mutter.

Mrs. Carsen started to walk back toward the house. Natalia turned to Tori. "What did you mean by that—'yeah, studying'?" she asked.

Tori raised her eyebrows. "Never mind, Nat," she said. "You'll find out soon enough!"

Tori hurried into the house after her mother. Natalia stared after her. Her new "family" certainly was going to take some getting used to!

3

Natalia's eyes flew open. She had been sound asleep. Something had awakened her. A loud noise, or . . .

She froze. The bedroom window was wide open. Natalia was certain she'd closed it before going to bed. As she stared into the darkness, she saw a dark form. Someone was climbing in the window!

Natalia felt a jolt of fear. She clutched the blanket to her chest. A thief! She couldn't believe it! Her first night in a new place, and a thief was breaking into her room!

She couldn't move. Her heart began racing. Should she pretend to be asleep? Would he leave her alone? There was a phone in the room, wasn't there? Yes—she was sure of it. She could jump up, run to the phone, and call the police. But could she finish the call in time? And what was the right phone number?

"Hey there, sleepyhead!" the intruder called.

It was a girl! Natalia gaped as the girl quietly closed the window and turned toward Natalia.

The thief wasn't a thief at all, but a teenage girl!

"You must be Natalia. I'm Veronica," the girl said. "Welcome to the good ole U.S.A.!" Veronica snapped on a small night-light, and the room was lit by a soft glow.

Natalia nearly giggled with relief. Veronica was pretty, with auburn hair cut in a dramatic style.

She was dressed in a pair of tight black leather pants and a silver-gray suede jacket. Natalia's gaze dropped to Veronica's feet, and she noticed with amusement that she only had on socks. Veronica followed her gaze. She grinned, then unzipped her jacket and pulled out a pair of gray suede high-heeled boots.

"You can't climb trees in high heels," she explained, tossing the boots on the floor.

Natalia did giggle now. The whole scene was unbelievable!

"Aren't you even going to say hi, roommate?" Veronica asked.

"Uh, hi," Natalia said. "You surprised me. I thought you were robbing the house or something."

"Sorry about that," Veronica said. "I didn't mean

to scare you, but it's a little too late to use the front door."

Natalia glanced at the clock. "Three forty-five," she read.

"Wow," Veronica said. "It's even later than I thought. I usually get in by three or so. This must be a new record for me." Veronica slipped off her jacket and brushed some dead leaves off the back. She hung the jacket carefully in the closet.

"You do this very often?" Natalia asked.

"Just when I want to be with my friends at night," Veronica answered. "We all sneak out so we can hang out together. I don't know if Corinne told you," she went on, "but the curfew around here is eleven o'clock." She shook her head in disbelief. "I stayed out later than that when I was in sixth grade! Most of the good parties don't even start until ten. Lucky for me, that tree is just outside the window. Come here," she said, pushing the window open again. "I'll show you."

Natalia slipped out of bed and joined Veronica at the window. She peered down in the dark, trying to see the ground. "It's awfully far down," she said.

"So? It's easy. All you have to do is climb out on that branch, the closest one," Veronica said, pointing. "From there it's practically like climbing a ladder. You just have to drop a few feet to get to the ground. And coming up is even easier. I pushed the storm window up a long time ago, so all you have to do is slide open the other window. Feel free to use it whenever you like," Veronica offered. "It's just one of the tricks I can teach you. You'll need plenty to survive the Carsen–Arnold household."

"Will I?" Natalia asked. She shivered from the cold and Veronica shut the window again.

"So," Veronica said, sitting down on her bed. "This will be great, having a roommate. You can cover for me, and I can cover for you." She crossed her feet under her. "Or you could come with me sometime. As a matter of fact, there's another party tomorrow night. You want to go and meet my friends?"

Natalia got back into bed and slid her legs under the blanket. She shook her head. "I can't," she said. "I have practice at five-thirty almost every day. If I don't get enough sleep, I won't be able to skate well." She glanced at the clock and groaned. "I have to get up in less than an hour!"

Veronica groaned, too. "Oh, no!" she exclaimed. "Not another one! Don't tell me you're just like Tori and her little friends? A total skating nut!"

Natalia grinned. "Well, I am a skater like Tori, and we'll be practicing at the same times."

"Ugh," Veronica said. "Not that I have anything against skating," she added quickly. "But the hours these people keep! Does that mean you'll be going to bed at nine o'clock, too?"

"I'm afraid so," Natalia said. Her brow furrowed.

She hoped Veronica wouldn't be waking her up every night like this. How would she ever have the energy to skate?

"Oh, well." Veronica shrugged. "Maybe you won't get to meet my friends, then. But it's still good to have a roommate." She stood up and pulled a nightgown out of her dresser drawer, then turned back to Natalia. "I bet this works out great," she said. "We'll watch out for each other. You can help me, and I'll help you." She smiled.

Natalia smiled back. Veronica had some wild habits, but at least she was friendlier than Tori.

"Uh, listen," Veronica said. "If Corinne asks you what time I got in tonight—I mean, last night—tell her it was eleven. I think she's getting a little suspicious," Veronica added. "But she'll believe me if you back me up."

Natalia hesitated. "I don't know, I . . ." she began.

"Look, it's no big deal," Veronica urged. "It's just a little white lie. All I'm doing is missing out on a little sleep to be with my friends. It's not like we're doing anything terrible. It's silly of Corinne and Roger to be so strict about curfews. Besides," she added with a frown, "if Corinne finds out, she'll send me back to live with my mother. And there's no way I would ever do that."

"No?" Natalia asked.

"No," Veronica said.

Natalia was silent for a moment, considering. She

didn't want to lie to Corinne. But Veronica might turn out to be the best friend Natalia had around here. Besides, it was exciting, plotting with Veronica.

"Okay," Natalia said.

"Great!" Veronica brightened. "So it's our secret, right?"

"Right," Natalia answered.

4

Natalia stifled a yawn as she followed Tori through the lobby of the ice rink. Only two hours had passed since Veronica woke her up. Natalia had just fallen asleep again when her alarm went off. She forced herself to get out of bed and get ready for practice. She hoped the lack of sleep wouldn't ruin the session.

Ahead of her, Tori pushed open the door to the locker room. Natalia hurried to catch up.

"Hi, everybody!" Tori called to a group of girls. Natalia had met all of Tori's friends at practice the day before. Now she looked from one to the next, trying to remember their names.

She knew Martina was the dark-haired girl who skated singles. And Haley was the bouncy redhead with sparkling green eyes. Haley skated pairs. Natalia thought hard. The slender brunet who also skated pairs was . . . Nikki, she remembered. And, of course, there was Amber. Natalia grinned. How could she forget her?

Natalia found an empty locker next to Tori's. She began to get changed. Next to her, Tori pulled a deep blue velvet skating dress out of her bag and shook it out. It was every bit as beautiful as the dress Tori had worn the day before, with lace trim across the bodice, long sleeves trimmed with still more lace, and a softly ruffled skirt.

Natalia stared at the dress in amazement. Did Tori wear such fancy clothes every day? she wondered.

Nikki caught the look. "Don't mind Tori," she told Natalia. "She always dresses like that," she said. "It's because her mom is a designer, with her own boutiques at Arnold Department Stores."

"Yes, I know about that," Natalia said politely. "The stores are owned by Tori's stepfather, Roger. I met him last night."

Natalia thought Roger was very nice, very friendly. And maybe easier to talk to than Tori's mother, Corinne. Corinne was so strict about everything. And she was always giving Tori advice about her skating.

"Well, Mom says I should always look as good as I can when I'm skating," Tori remarked.

Natalia pulled up her practice tights and smoothed her simple black skating dress. "My clothes—they are okay?" she whispered to Nikki.

"Sure," Nikki said. She nodded at the others. Natalia saw that Amber was wearing leggings and a sweatshirt again. So was Haley. And Nikki and Martina wore skating dresses as simple as her own. Natalia breathed a little sigh of relief. It was hard enough trying to fit into a new place. Wearing the wrong clothes would just make things more difficult.

Tori zipped her dress and straightened the trim at her neck. "It works, you know? If you're going to be a champion, you've got to dress like a champion," she declared.

"And work like a champion," Nikki offered.

"And eat like a champion," Haley put in.

"And sleep like a champion," Martina added.

The girls started giggling. "And comb your hair like a champion," Amber offered.

"And brush your teeth like a champion . . ."

"And take showers like a champion . . ."

"Spoken like true champions!" Tori finished. They all burst out laughing.

Natalia grinned. She couldn't help envying them a little. They seemed to get along so well. She thought of her own friends back home with a little pang. Would she ever feel like one of this group of friends?

The laughter died down as everyone finished

dressing. Natalia sat on the bench to pull on her skates.

Nikki sat next to her. "So, Natalia, how was your Silver Blades tryout?" she asked. "Pretty tough, huh? Did they make you do your long and your short programs?"

"And footwork sequences?" Haley added.

"And every jump ever invented?" Martina joked.

Natalia frowned. "Tryout? What tryout?" she asked.

Nikki seemed confused. "You know, the audition. Didn't Kathy and Dan make you do a bunch of jumps and spins and stuff before they let you join Silver Blades?"

Natalia hesitated. Nikki and Tori and their friends waited for her answer. Natalia noticed that some other girls in the locker room also grew quiet. They stopped their conversations to listen to her.

"Um, no," she said finally. "They didn't ask me to do any of those things."

"That's funny," Nikki said. "They never let anybody into Silver Blades without a really tough tryout."

"Well, we sent a letter from my old coach," Natalia explained. "And tapes of my skating."

"Oh!" Martina said. "I guess since you came from so far away, they just used the tapes as your tryout."

"I guess. Because no one said anything about having to audition once I got here," Natalia said.

"You're lucky," Nikki said. "I still remember how nervous I was at my tryout. I was sure I'd blown it."

The others chimed in, comparing their tryout experiences, and soon the noise level in the room returned to normal.

Natalia was silent. She didn't like the resentful looks some of the girls—not Tori and her friends—were giving her. Natalia was sure they were talking about her. But Martina was right, Natalia reassured herself. They made an exception for her because she came from so far away.

She finished dressing and hurried out to the rink. She and the others quickly did some off-ice warm-ups. Then they stepped onto the ice.

As Natalia pushed off, she forgot all about tryouts and being tired. She was lost in the familiar movements. So lost that she was startled when Dan Trapp's voice broke into her thoughts.

"All right, kids, gather 'round!" he called.

Natalia half expected to see a megaphone in his hand, Dan's voice was so loud. She joined Tori, Amber, and the rest of the Silver Blades members as they grouped around Dan.

"I'd like to introduce you all to our newest member—Natalia Cherkas," Dan announced. Dan motioned to Natalia to join him at the front of the group, and she skated to his side. He put an arm around her shoulder. Natalia felt herself blush with embarrassment as everyone stared at her.

"Natalia came all the way from Moscow," Dan

went on. "She's a talented, lovely skater. I know she'll challenge all of you to skate your best. Let's all give her a warm welcome to Silver Blades!"

The kids clapped. "Thank you," Natalia said, "I am very happy to be here." Dan gave her a pat on the shoulder, and then she skated back to stand near Tori. Dan said she was a member of Silver Blades. So that must mean she didn't have to try out again.

"Now, back to business," Dan said. "Today we'll do a special exercise. We'll tap into the hidden energy reserves each of you has right in here." Dan pointed to his chest. "But to reach in and open that fountain of energy we have to start here." He tapped a finger to his forehead. "So put on your skate guards, everyone, and follow me."

Natalia looked around, bewildered. What was Dan talking about? Why were they leaving the ice? She thought they were going to skate this morning! She looked at Tori, but Tori just shrugged.

Natalia slipped on her skate guards and followed Dan and the others to the ballet room. Perhaps, Natalia thought, they were going to practice ballet exercises? But Dan didn't teach ballet.

"Okay," Dan said when they were all gathered in the ballet room. "Take off your skates and line up across the room."

When everyone was ready, Dan stood in front of the group. "Now each one of you will learn how to become an energy magnet."

A ripple of giggles passed through the group, but

no one protested. Natalia was puzzled. Energy mag-
nets? It sounded more like science class than a skating exercise!

"All right. Let's spread out a little here, so you
have enough room to move your arms and legs
freely," Dan instructed. "That's good. Now close
your eyes and take four or five slow, deep breaths.
Allow yourself to get nice and relaxed. Now imagine
that all the energy inside you is squeezed into a tiny
ball. Can you feel the ball resting in the center of
your body?"

Natalia opened one eye just enough to see several
kids nodding their heads. She tried to picture what
Dan was talking about inside of her, but she
couldn't feel a thing.

"Good," Dan continued. "Now I want you to
move that energy ball . . . slowly, now . . .
throughout your body. Picture it flowing just like the
blood flows through your veins, moving smoothly
from one place to another. As the ball rolls from one
place to the next, you'll feel that part of your body
lift with the energy. If you're doing it right, I should
actually be able to see the energy flowing through
your body," Dan said.

Natalia peeked at the others again. She saw a girl
named Rebecca standing nearby. Rebecca was shift-
ing her weight from foot to foot and frowning with
concentration.

"Let's take it to the right hand," Dan said.

Natalia copied the way Rebecca lifted her right arm.

"Here it goes . . . into your right shoulder . . . to your right elbow . . . and down to your hand," Dan went on.

Natalia was sure no one could see the energy moving through her body. She didn't feel a thing.

Dan talked on, moving the energy ball from one place to another. The room was quiet except for his voice. Everyone but Natalia seemed totally into the exercise.

"All right, kids," Dan finally said. "I want you to practice on your own, on the ice and off. When you're on the ice today, try to imagine that energy ball moving along with you. Let it pull you through your routines. Pretty soon you'll be able to feel it moving through you at all times."

The group began to break up. Everyone was talking with excitement.

"That was so cool!" Amber said. "I really felt something moving inside me."

"You would," Tori said, rolling her eyes.

"You mean you didn't, Tori?" asked a tall red-headed girl.

"Well, I felt something, Diana," Tori admitted. "Just not as much as Dan said we would."

"Dan's exercises always work for me," Diana told her.

Several other kids were chatting about what the

energy ball felt like to them. Natalia seemed to be
the only one who hadn't felt anything. She kept her
head down. She was relieved that no one asked her
how she felt.

She was glad to remove her skate guards and step
back onto the ice. This was where skating lessons
were supposed to happen, not in a ballet room!

Natalia performed her warm-up and then ran
through her current routine. Finally it was time for
her lesson. She skated over to Dan, ready to begin.
She couldn't wait to get down to some real coach-
ing.

"All right, Natalia," Dan said. "I saw you running
through your routine. I'd like to see you skate it to
your music."

Dan skated to the side of the rink and slipped a
cassette into the tape player. Natalia skated to center ice and assumed her beginning pose. The first
notes of her music began, and she glided into her
opening moves.

Her program went smoothly, until she got to the
double axel again. She told herself to relax, it was
silly to miss one of the first jumps she ever learned.
She held her breath as she launched into the move.
Oh no! she thought. Not again! Her double turned
into a single. She finished the rest of the program,
then skated back to Dan.

She was embarrassed again. But at least Dan
would show her what she was doing wrong.

"Very nice!" Dan said. "Your spins are truly elegant, and I'm very pleased at the quality of your jumps. As I see it, our focus is on developing your artistry. I'd like to see you express the inner you on the ice. The exercise with energy balls should help. It's a very exciting concept."

Natalia waited for Dan to say more. He smiled at her.

"But—what about my double axel?" Natalia asked.

"Oh, I'm sure that will come," Dan said. "Another thing we should work on is building up speed. The thing that stops most people from going fast enough is a lack of self-confidence. You can work on that up here." Dan tapped her forehead with his index finger.

Natalia stared at him. "But—won't you show me the double axel?" she asked.

"Not now. Just make sure your knees are deeply bent when you're stroking," Dan said. "Follow through to a straight leg before you let your leg leave the ice. And concentrate on making every move smooth—no bouncing up and down in the torso."

Natalia listened carefully. "I think I understand. But, can you show me?"

"Oh, and thinking about that energy ball will help," Dan added as if he hadn't heard. "Move it around as you're stroking, nice and smooth. When you get more speed going, the jump will come much easier. All right?" he asked.

"Uh, sure," Natalia said.

"Good. Focus on that, then, and I'll touch base with you in a little while." With that, Dan turned and skated away.

Focus on what? Energy balls? Stroking? Natalia stared after Dan, totally confused. In Moscow her coaches never talked so much. They showed her how to do each move, and she copied their form, their technique.

Maybe Dan didn't have any technique, she thought. Maybe he couldn't even skate that well! And if he couldn't skate, how could he ever show her what to do?

Natalia ran through her routine again, and then again. She wasn't sure exactly what Dan wanted her to do, but she tried bending her knees. She even tried thinking about energy balls. The time went slowly.

Natalia circled the rink again and noticed Tori leaving the ice. Natalia checked the clock and frowned. But they had another fifteen minutes of practice time! America was a crazy place, Natalia thought. The coaches wasted time talking about energy balls. And the skaters here were just plain lazy!

Natalia felt more discouraged than ever. She ran through her routine again. But she didn't even bother attempting the double axel. She just left it out. What was the point? She couldn't fix it on her own. She just wouldn't try it at all, she decided. Not until Dan started acting like a real coach. But how soon would that be?

5

Natalia twirled the combination lock for the third time. "It still will not open!" she cried in disgust.

"I'll do it, Nat," Tori said impatiently. She nudged Natalia out of the way and spun the lock. Natalia's locker swung open immediately.

Natalia stashed her jacket and skate bag in the locker. She didn't have any books to put in it yet. It was Monday morning and her first day at Kent Academy, the private school Tori and Haley also attended.

Natalia was nervous. She was grateful she had Tori and Haley to show her around. She hadn't even gone to school back home. Instead she had private tutors. This school was so big! Kids streamed by in all directions, talking and laughing, their arms full of books. She'd never seen so many kids in one place before.

Tori checked Natalia's schedule. "Your first class is math in room one-o-seven. It's down there." Tori pointed to the right. She and Natalia started down the hall together. Suddenly Tori stopped in her tracks.

"Wait! I almost forgot." Tori searched through her purse. She pulled out a small piece of paper. "I've got to get this note signed by the nurse. I missed a couple of classes the other day," she explained. "I was really tired, so I went home and slept all afternoon. The nurse's office is in the other direction. You'll have to find your class by yourself."

"But I can't! I . . ." Natalia began to say.

"It's easy," Tori assured her. "Just go down this hall, take a right at the next corridor, and follow that around to the left." She stuffed the schedule into Natalia's hand and then hurried off.

Natalia stared after Tori. Then she hurried down the hall. She turned left at the next corridor and walked to the end. Oh, no, she thought. Tori said to turn right!

A bell rang, and the hall suddenly emptied. Natalia was the only one still wandering around. She went back in the other direction and started over. Finally she reached room 107. She took a deep breath and opened the door.

"Good morning, Ms. Cherkas. You *are* Ms. Cherkas, aren't you?" the teacher's voice boomed out. Natalia saw a short, round man peering at her over his glasses.

"Yes. I'm Natalia Cherkas."

"How kind of you to join us. I am Mr. Grossman." Mr. Grossman made a great show of checking the time on his watch. "As you can see, this class has already started. I don't know how you do things in Russia, but here at Kent Academy, we expect our students to make it to class at the proper time. But since this is your first day, I won't mark you late."

Natalia felt the heat rising in her face. "Yes, sir," she mumbled. She spotted an empty desk on the far side of the room and headed for it. She sat down and tried to ignore the curious looks she was getting.

Luckily Mr. Grossman paid no attention to her for the rest of the class. She breathed a sigh of relief when it was over. She checked her schedule again. English was next. Oh, no! She had to go completely back in the other direction!

Natalia raced out of the room and hurried through the crowded hallways.

"Natalia, over here!" Haley called across the cafeteria. Natalia smiled when she saw her. Haley was dressed in tight red leggings, a big yellow T-shirt, and a colorful tie-dyed vest. Natalia hurried to stand in line behind her.

"Hi, Nat! Are you having hot lunch or cold?" Haley asked.

"Cold, I guess," Natalia said. "It would be nice to have a big, crispy salad."

"Oh! Then you have to get on the other line," Haley told her. She pointed to a long line a few feet away.

"Okay," Natalia said. She moved into the other line. She picked up a container of juice and a yogurt, but she couldn't find the salads anywhere. Natalia paid the cashier and searched for Haley. She spotted her at a table with Tori and hurried to join them.

"Sit down, Nat," Tori said. She nodded at the yogurt. "Is that all you're having?" she asked. She bit into a big tuna-fish sandwich.

Natalia pulled out a chair and sat down. "Well, I wanted to buy a salad, but I didn't see any," she said.

"Oops." Haley made a face. "When I said cold lunch, I meant a lunch you brought from home. I thought you only wanted a juice with it. Hot lunch is what you buy here . . . whether it's a salad or a hamburger." Haley laughed.

Natalia felt embarrassed. "Well, where do I go to buy a salad, then?"

Tori glanced up at the cafeteria clock, and then at the line in front of the food area. "Forget it," she said. "There's only about five minutes left to this lunch period. You don't have time to stand in line again."

"Here," Haley said. "Take this." She held up the half of her sandwich that was still uneaten and offered it to Natalia.

Natalia smiled. "Thank you, but I couldn't take your lunch," she said politely. In Russia it was considered rude to accept such an offer the first time. But the second or even the third time Haley offered, Natalia would say yes. The sandwich looked delicious.

But to Natalia's astonishment, Haley shrugged and took a huge bite out of the sandwich. "How was your morning?" she asked.

Natalia's stomach rumbled, but she ignored it. She tried not to look at Haley's sandwich. "Um, not so great," she said. She opened her yogurt and gulped down a few spoonfuls. "I was late for math—and English," Natalia said. "I found my other classes okay."

"Well, Nat, don't forget it's your first day. Who's your math teacher?" Tori asked.

Natalia flinched at the nickname "Nat." But she answered politely. "I have Mr. Grossman for math," she said.

"Oh, that is bad," Haley said. "Everyone knows he's a total creep. Don't let him get to you."

"Who do you have for English?" Tori asked.

"Mrs. Corvina," Natalia answered.

"She's really nice," Haley said. "Not like Gross-man."

"I guess. But . . ." Natalia hesitated.

"But what?" Tori asked.

"Oh, nothing . . . it was just kind of embarrass-ing. In her class, I mean . . ." Natalia began.

"What happened?" Haley asked.

"I asked someone where the bin was," Natalia said.

"The bin? What's that?" Haley frowned.

"It's where you throw your garbage. I think you call it a wastebasket. But I was taught 'bin'—that's how they say it in England," Natalia explained. "Anyway, everyone laughed at me. And then some boy said the whole school was one big loony bin, and everyone laughed even more."

"Loony bin!" Haley hooted.

Tori started laughing, too, and Natalia felt her cheeks burning in embarrassment again. "That is exactly what the class did," she told them.

Haley blinked in surprise. "Hey," she said, "we're not laughing at you—" she started to say. But just then another bell rang.

"World's shortest lunch break," Haley said. "Time to go!" She leaped up and gathered her books together.

Natalia pulled out her wrinkled schedule again.

"Where you off to next?" Tori asked.

"Chemistry with Mr. Axelson. Room two twenty-four," Natalia read. She looked up. "Where is that?"

"Second floor, east corridor," Tori told her. "Haley, aren't you going that way?"

Natalia thought Haley hesitated before she answered. "Sure," Haley said. "Come on, Nat. I'll show you where it is."

The girls rushed out of the cafeteria. Tori went off in one direction and Haley led Natalia the other way, toward a stairwell. They started up, when a tall blond girl stopped them.

"Hey, Haley!" the tall girl said. "Where do you think you're going?"

"Hi, Kim," Haley said. "I'm going to English, of course."

"But we're meeting in the library today, remember? To work on our term papers?" Kim asked.

"Uh-oh," Haley said. "You're right. I forgot all about that. And my notes are in my locker! I'd better go get them." Haley looked anxiously at her watch, and then at Natalia. "I'll never make it if I take you to your class, Nat."

"But . . ." Natalia felt a burst of panic.

"Don't worry," Haley said. She glanced at the kids streaming past. She reached out and grabbed a stocky brunet by the arm. "Cynthia!" she said. "Do me a favor?"

"I guess," Cynthia answered.

"This is Natalia," Haley said quickly. "She's new,

and she doesn't know her way around. Show her where Mr. Axelson's chem class is, okay?"

"Okay," Cynthia said. "Come on, Natalia."

Natalia gaped as Haley rushed down the stairs with Kim. She swallowed hard. She had counted on Tori and Haley helping her to feel at home. Instead she felt like an abandoned animal that nobody wanted. She felt lonely and scared, and mad at herself for feeling that way.

"Well, come on, Natalie," Cynthia called as she headed up the stairs again. "We'll both be late!"

Natalia ignored the way Cynthia mispronounced her name. Maybe nobody in Seneca Hills knew how to say "Natalia"! She rushed up the stairs behind Cynthia and then down a long corridor.

"Hey, Cynthia!" someone called. A tall boy grabbed Cynthia by the arm. "Emergency! Private talk, okay?"

Cynthia turned to Natalia. "Sorry," she said. "Got to go. But you'll find two twenty-four—it's that way." Cynthia pointed down the hall, and then she and her friend were gone.

Natalia stared after them a moment. Then she took a deep breath and plunged into the crowd, dodging the flow of bodies that pushed past her. The way everyone bumped and jostled her, she felt invisible. Angry tears welled up in her eyes, but she blinked them away.

Could she survive this awful school—all on her own?

6

"**H**ey, Patrick, catch!" Alex Beekman picked up a pink ballet shoe and tossed it through the air. Natalia remembered that Alex was Nikki's pairs partner. He was fifteen, with curly dark hair and a dimpled smile.

"Got it!" Patrick McGuire yelled back. He caught the shoe and waved it above his head. Patrick was also fifteen. He was Haley's pairs partner, and Natalia thought he looked just like Haley, with his bright red hair and bright green eyes.

"Give me that, you turkey-brain!" Haley squealed. Haley leaped toward Patrick, jumping up and down as she tried to grab his arm to get back the ballet slipper.

"You need this, partner?" Patrick asked in pretend innocence.

"Of course I need it!" Haley shrieked. "Ms. Beaumont will be here any minute!"

It was Tuesday afternoon, and a group of the older Silver Blades members was gathered in the ballet room for their weekly lesson. Patrick dropped the ballet slipper and hoisted Haley into an overhead lift.

"Now you're up and it's down," Patrick joked.

Martina scooped up the slipper. "I've got it, Haley, don't worry," she called, laughing.

Up in the air, Haley giggled. Patrick twirled her around twice, then brought her back down to the floor. Haley broke away, still laughing.

"I'll get you later," she warned Patrick and Alex.

Natalia watched from a corner of the room. All around her the other Silver Blades members waited in groups of two or three. They were talking or laughing at the show Haley and the boys were putting on. Natalia was the only one waiting alone. She bent over and pretended to adjust her ballet slipper. That way, no one could see her face.

Ms. Beaumont entered the room, and the class suddenly became quiet. "All right, class." Ms. Beaumont reached up and tucked a stray piece of her long brown hair into the bun at the back of her head. She was small and slender, but the muscles in her legs were well-defined. She walked with her toes slightly turned out. She looked exactly like a ballet teacher ought to look, Natalia thought.

Ms. Beaumont put on a tape of music. "Time for

barre exercises," she announced. She walked over to Natalia. "You should find this routine familiar," she said. "I know you had intense ballet training in Moscow."

Natalia nodded and found a place at the long wooden barre that ran along one side of the room, in front of full-length mirrors.

Ms. Beaumont took her place at the front of the class. The students' eyes were pinned on her as she led them through a series of basic ballet exercises. Natalia lost herself in the familiar motions. She enjoyed the feeling of her body moving to the music.

"Beautiful, Natalia!" Ms. Beaumont called out. "Your placement is excellent." Ms. Beaumont stopped and clapped her hands. "Attention, class! I want you all to see this," she announced. She walked over to Natalia and placed her index finger between Natalia's shoulder blades.

"You see how her body is perfectly aligned? The hips are even, the back is straight, the head is up." Ms. Beaumont placed her finger under Natalia's chin, raising her head a fraction of an inch.

"Your formal ballet training certainly shows," Ms. Beaumont told Natalia. "Now, class," she went on, "this is the position you want to achieve. Just like Natalia's." Ms. Beaumont left Natalia and placed her hand on Nikki's back. "Not like this. Your whole back is so tense! Relax, Nikki, like Natalia. Pretend you are suspended by a thread at the top of the head."

Ms. Beaumont turned away from Nikki. Natalia saw Nikki's face grow bright red. Nikki dropped her eyes.

"Let me see the position again, now, all of you," Ms. Beaumont ordered. "Try to imitate the beautiful placement that Natalia has."

Natalia noticed a few of the girls staring at her. She shifted her position, feeling self-conscious. She thought she heard some kids whispering about her. Natalia dropped her own eyes.

They went on to do floor work, and then combinations of moves and a series of leaps. Finally the class was over, and everyone headed for the locker rooms. As she walked, Natalia heard a voice ring out behind her.

"I guess Nikki's not the best ballet dancer around here anymore," someone said.

Natalia turned her head sharply. She thought the girl named Diana had said it. Natalia glanced at Nikki, who was walking just a few feet away from her. Nikki's head was down. Natalia couldn't tell if Nikki heard the comment or not.

Natalia felt terrible. She hadn't meant to show off, or to make Nikki feel bad. She hadn't even known that Nikki was considered the best dancer in ballet class.

The girls filed into the locker room. A lot of the girls, who Natalia didn't know, began changing into their street clothes. But Natalia, along with Tori and her group of friends, had their skating lessons now.

They all slipped off their leotards and tights and changed into leggings and sweatshirts. Tori, of course, pulled a lovely pink skating dress from her locker.

"Great class, huh?" Tori asked Natalia as she adjusted the dress. "Ms. Beaumont was really impressed with you."

"Yes, but Nikki—" Natalia began. She wanted to say something about how badly she felt about Nikki.

"Oh, I don't think Nikki enjoyed it much, huh, Nik?" Haley interrupted. "How does it feel *not* to be teacher's pet anymore?" Haley teased.

Natalia glanced at Nikki, who blushed slightly. "I feel fine. Forget it, Haley," Nikki said quietly.

Haley jumped up on the bench next to her locker. She stuck her nose up in the air and turned her toes out, walking in mincing little steps. Natalia felt a shock of recognition. Haley was doing a perfect imitation of Ms. Beaumont! Tori, Martina, and Amber all started giggling. Even Nikki giggled.

"Now zis is zee perfect example of zee *changement des pieds*," Haley said. She jumped up in the air, pointed her toes, crossed her feet, and landed. "And Natalia, she ees zee best dancer . . . soo lovely . . . soo be-oo-ti-ful. Because zee Russians, you know, do zee ballet soo bee-oo-ti-ful-ly," Haley finished.

Natalia swallowed. It was funny, but it also made her feel very uncomfortable.

Nikki gave Haley a little shove. "Cut it out," she said.

"Oh, come on," Haley said. "Admit it—you were jealous. It was written all over your face. Now that Natalia's here, you're just a klutz like the rest of us," Haley teased.

Nikki glanced at Natalia, then made a face at Haley. "I'll never be a klutz like you, Haley. You're the worst!" she said.

"Nikki," Natalia said, "I'm sorry about ballet class. I didn't mean to—"

"Forget it," Nikki said. "It's not your fault. You didn't do anything."

"But . . ." Natalia said, "it's not such a big deal, what Ms. Beaumont was telling you to do. It's really easy, you know." She pointed to Nikki's shoulders. "You're just a little stiff there," she said.

Nikki frowned. "I said forget it." She started searching for something in her locker, hiding her face from Natalia.

Natalia took a step backward. She'd made a mistake. She hadn't made things better, just worse. She felt as if everything she did in America turned out all wrong!

She turned silently back to her locker to finish changing. Suddenly she heard voices whispering as some of the other girls left the locker room. ". . . special treatment . . ." she heard, and then, ". . . not fair . . . tryouts . . . how dare she." Were they talking about her? She stared after them, but she couldn't tell who had spoken. There were too many conversations going on at once.

Haley interrupted Natalia's thoughts as she addressed their little group. "Hey, you guys," she said, "you want to come to my house on Saturday night? The 'Stars on Ice' special is on TV. My mom said it's okay. I was going to ask Alex and Patrick, too."

"Sure," Nikki said. She looked at Haley, avoiding Natalia's eyes.

"Sounds good to me," Martina said.

"Sounds like fun," Tori said. "We can make it, too, can't we, Nat?" She turned and looked straight at Natalia.

Haley and Nikki were watching her, too. Natalia hesitated. She wasn't sure what to do. She didn't think Nikki really wanted her hanging around. But Tori was smiling and nodding at her.

Natalia nodded, too. She'd go to Haley's house with the others and pretend she belonged. Even though she didn't.

"Of course," Natalia said, forcing herself to sound more enthusiastic than she felt. "I'd love to go."

7

Two hours later, Natalia stepped off the ice. She slipped her skate guards over her blades and stomped toward the locker room. She was so frustrated, she wanted to scream! Her lessons with Dan were getting her absolutely nowhere.

She still couldn't land her double axel. She had two-footed the landing about twenty times. She asked Dan for help, over and over. But what did he say? She needed to visualize it! To see it in her head. Natalia clenched her fists. That wasn't the problem. She could see it in her head. She just couldn't do it!

She was so tired of Dan and all his talk about inner strength and energy balls and learning to express herself. Why couldn't he be more like her coach back home? Like a real coach, who showed you exactly what to do? That was how she worked in Russia. Her coach would do the move, then Natalia would copy as best she could, over and over and over. Finally she would get it perfectly. If only Dan would—

Natalia heard someone calling her name. She turned to see a tall, red-haired woman headed her way.

"Natalia," the woman called. "I need to speak with you, dear."

Natalia stopped walking, and the woman caught up with her. "You remember me, don't you? I'm Mrs. Bowen," she said, holding out her hand. "The president of Silver Blades."

"Of course, I remember," Natalia said. She had met Mrs. Bowen in person her first day at the rink. "I'm very pleased to see you again," she said in the polite manner she had been taught to use with adults.

"Listen, dear," Mrs. Bowen said, "I'm afraid we have a small problem. There have been some complaints."

Natalia's smile faded. "Complaints?"

"Yes. It's not a problem, really. But there are some members who feel that we made too much of an exception for you, in the way you joined Silver Blades." Mrs. Bowen patted Natalia on the arm, as if to offer reassurance. "Not that you aren't a wonderful skater. It's just that, normally, one only gets

accepted to the club after going through a very difficult tryout. Some people feel you aren't yet an official member of the club.''

Natalia was stunned. "But . . . I thought I was a
member already. And I did try out. We sent you
tapes,'' she protested. "And a letter from my coach.
Dan said—''

"Yes, yes, I know, dear,'' Mrs. Bowen said, pat-
ting her arm again. "And your tapes were fine. But
this all has to do with the rules of the club,'' she
explained. "I've gone over them, and I'm afraid
there's just no way around it. If we let you in without an official tryout, we'll be opening the door to
all kinds of trouble.''

"But, my father—'' Natalia began. Mrs. Bowen
interrupted her again.

"Rules are rules,'' she said firmly. "And, really,
we are making an exception for you. Normally we
hold large tryouts twice a year, drawing many,
many skaters for just a few openings,'' she explained. She bent her head closer to Natalia's. "But
I think, considering the circumstances, we can bend
the rules just a little. So I've set a date. I'd wanted to
do this right away, but unfortunately it will be two
weeks before Kathy Bart, Dan Trapp, and I will be
available at the same time.''

"What will I have to do?'' Natalia asked.

"Your regular program will be fine,'' Mrs. Bowen
told her. "I'm sure it contains all the required jumps

and spins. Don't worry, you won't have any problems."

Natalia stared at Mrs. Bowen. She could feel panic rising in her throat. She *would* have problems. She couldn't land her double axel, and she was sure that was one of the required jumps she would have to do in her tryout.

Since she'd been in America, her skating had gone downhill in every way. She felt it every time she stepped onto the ice. Her form wasn't nearly as precise as it had been. At home she had ballet class three or four times a week, not just once like they did at Silver Blades. No matter what Ms. Beaumont said, Natalia didn't feel as if her form was wonderful. It felt sloppy and soft.

And the rest of her skating felt softer, too. She didn't have the same kind of energy she used to have. She used to take off into a jump and feel as though she could add extra revolutions. Now she felt as if she had to force herself to complete the required moves.

That was Dan's fault, Natalia thought. He wasn't anything like the kind of coach she was used to. He didn't know how to show her anything, and he left her almost alone on the ice. At home her coach made her repeat her moves, one at a time, over and over. Then she would put the moves together, and only then, when her coach was satisfied, was she allowed to skate the entire program.

Dan just told her to practice. He didn't say which moves to practice. Natalia felt more and more discouraged—

"How is two weeks from today?" Mrs. Bowen asked, interrupting her thoughts. "Right after morning practice?"

"Oh. Yes, that's fine," Natalia said, thinking, What difference did it make, anyway?

"Good. I'll be looking forward to it," Mrs. Bowen said, and walked away.

Natalia moved slowly toward the locker room, feeling as if someone had kicked her in the stomach. She couldn't believe it. As if things weren't bad enough already!

Her new coach was a disaster. Her new school was a disaster. She didn't fit in at home, either. Veronica still kept crazy hours, and Mrs. Carsen didn't seem to know what was going on. Several times Natalia woke up to the sound of teenagers giggling outside her window. Veronica didn't seem to care that she was disturbing Natalia's sleep.

And Veronica was messy, too. Horribly messy! Natalia had to clean up after her just to find a place to sit or read or study. As for Tori, Natalia couldn't quite figure her out. Some days she was friendly, but other times she seemed to resent Natalia just for being around. And she was very competitive on the ice.

And now this! A tryout, when Natalia's skating was at its all-time worst!

She could just imagine the tryout. Everyone would laugh at her skating, just as they'd been laughing at her ever since she got here.

What would happen if she failed the tryout? She could be kicked out of Silver Blades before she'd even gotten started! What would her father say? And how would she ever face Tori and her friends again? She'd be totally humiliated!

It's the end of my dream, Natalia thought. But she wasn't even sure it was her dream anymore.

8

"**M**om? We're home!" Tori called as she and Natalia pushed open the front door.

I wish, Natalia thought. I wish I really were home. In Moscow. What I'd give to feel at home again!

"I'm here, girls." Mrs. Carsen came out of the kitchen, holding a coffee mug. "I was just catching up on some paperwork upstairs." She laughed. "Sometimes I can't get anything done at the office."

Natalia felt a pang as she watched Tori kiss her mother on the cheek. She missed her father, her grandmother, and her sister, Jelena, so much!

"Too bad you didn't watch my practice today," Tori told her mother. "I was really doing well on

my new triple combination. I hit it just right—
twice."

"That's wonderful, Tori," Mrs. Carsen said. She
turned to Natalia. "And how did your day go?" she
asked.

"It was fine," Natalia lied. There was no point in
telling the truth.

"How are you getting along with Dan?" Mrs. Carsen asked. She took a sip of her coffee, peering at
Natalia over the rim of the cup.

"Mom, she's only been here a week," Tori protested. "Give her a break. It takes time to get used to
new stuff, and—"

"A week is long enough to get an impression of
things, Tori. I want to know what Natalia thinks,"
Mrs. Carsen insisted.

Natalia shifted uncomfortably from one foot to
the other. "Dan is . . . very interesting," she finally
said. "He seems like a nice man."

Mrs. Carsen beamed at her. "That's wonderful,
Natalia! I'm so glad things have started out well."

Natalia smiled politely. "Yes."

Mrs. Carsen glanced at her watch. "Isn't this the
time your father usually calls?" she asked.

"Yes," Natalia answered. Her father had called
her at night a few times over the past week. He
never had much time to talk. He was usually on
his way to a formal dinner or some work-related
event. Natalia looked forward to his phone calls, but

they also made her feel lonely. It seemed she would just get warmed up talking when he had to hang up.

"Why don't you use the phone in your bedroom?" Mrs. Carsen suggested. "That way you can have some privacy."

"Thank you," Natalia said. She went into the kitchen and grabbed a snack, then practically flew up to the room she shared with Veronica.

Veronica's clothes were strewn all over the room. As usual. She'd even left some of her things on Natalia's bed. Normally Natalia would have put them away carefully, but she was tired of cleaning up after her roommate. She swept the whole pile of clothing and books onto the floor. Let Veronica take care of it, she thought.

Natalia couldn't wait any longer for her father to call. She found her address book, then picked up the phone and sat on her bed. She carefully dialed her father's number at work. Luckily he was still in his office, and his secretary put her right through.

"Natalia! How are you?" he said in Russian.

Natalia suddenly felt tears welling up in her eyes. She couldn't let her father know how homesick she was, though. He was a practical man. He often said people should be ruled by reason, not emotion. And he expected Natalia to feel the same way.

"Hi, Papa. I'm fine," Natalia answered in Russian. "But I have something important to tell you." She took a deep breath, then plunged ahead. "We made a mistake. I shouldn't have come to America, after all.''

"Oh?" Mr. Cherkas sounded surprised. "Why do you say that?"

"Nothing is going the way it's supposed to," Natalia blurted out. "Dan Trapp isn't a good coach for me at all." Her voice started to tremble. Natalia fought to keep it steady. "I'm not learning anything, Papa!"

"But he was very highly recommended," Mr. Cherkas pointed out. "Marina said he was one of the best, and that you could learn a great deal from him."

"But I'm not," Natalia insisted. "He's completely different from Marina. She and I worked so well together. I don't even understand what Dan's talking about most of the time."

"Then you must listen more carefully," Mr. Cherkas said.

"But I *do* listen," Natalia complained. "He just doesn't make any sense."

"Natalia, I'm sure Mr. Trapp would not have such an excellent reputation if he made no sense." Mr. Cherkas spoke slowly and patiently, as if Natalia were a little child. "You've only worked with him for a week. You must give yourself and Mr. Trapp more time to build a relationship."

"But you don't understand," Natalia protested. Suddenly all her feelings and frustrations came out in a rush of words. "It's not just Dan. That's the worst part, because I'm falling so far behind in my skating." Natalia had to swallow before she could go on.

"But everything else is awful, too," she said. "I hate the school. It's big and unfriendly and confusing. And no one helps me there. I don't fit in and I have no friends. And I never will! I hate it here, Papa! I want to go home. *Now.*" A few tears ran down Natalia's cheeks. She wiped them away.

"Really, Natalia. You must not let your lonely feelings get the better of you," her father said.

There was a long pause. Natalia cried silently as she waited for her father to speak again.

"Natalia, you are wrong about one thing," he said in a softer voice. "I do understand. You forget that I have spent many, many days in other countries, far from home. I know what it's like to be the only foreigner in a group of people. But I have learned, Natalia, that it is possible to make friends, even with people who are very different from you. It may not be as easy as it is to form friendships at home, but you can do it. Just as you can learn to work with a coach you do not know well. You must be patient. This is just homesickness. It will pass, believe me," Mr. Cherkas finished.

Natalia took a deep, shaky breath and forced herself to stop crying. Her father didn't understand. Being patient was fine for him. He was a diplomat.

Patience was part of his job. But she didn't have time to work things out. Her skating was falling apart, and she was going to have to try out for Silver Blades in two weeks! She'd make a fool of herself in front of everyone.

"They're making me try out for Silver Blades," Natalia told her father. "Even though they said I was already in."

Mr. Cherkas laughed. "Really, Natalia," he said. "Is that what's worrying you? You should be happy to have the chance to show off for them. Let them see what a beautiful skater you are."

Natalia bit her lip. Her father was impossible. He had never been able to see her flaws on the ice. Even if she tried to explain to him that she might not measure up, he wouldn't believe her.

"Please, Papa," she tried one last time. "Won't you let me go home?"

"I'm sorry, Natalia," he said. "I can't let you do that. I understand that you're having a difficult time right now. But believe me, it will get better. You simply need to give it some time."

Natalia's heart sank. She was doomed. Her father would never change his mind. He would never agree to help her, and there was nothing she could do about it. Nothing.

"I'd better go now," she said. Her throat ached with the effort of holding back her tears.

Her father said good-bye, and Natalia hung up. She started to cry all over again.

The bedroom door opened. "Hey," Veronica called out. "Why are all my clothes on the floor? What's the big idea?"

"They were all over my bed," Natalia said. "I couldn't even find a place to sit down."

"Well, you didn't have to throw them on the floor! Some of those clothes cost a small fortune, you know," Veronica complained.

Natalia whirled around. "Then put them where they belong! I'm sick of cleaning up after you," she said. "I am not your maid."

"But . . ." Veronica took one look at Natalia's red eyes and tear-stained face and stopped. "Hey," she said. "What's the matter?"

"Nothing. It's nothing." Natalia rubbed her forehead with the back of her hand. She felt a headache coming on.

"It sure doesn't look like nothing." Veronica plucked a few tissues from the box on her dresser. She handed them to Natalia. "Did something happen at practice? Or school?"

Natalia wiped her nose. "At school . . . at practice . . . everywhere," she said. She couldn't help it. It all came spilling out.

"Tori and her friends don't like me," Natalia blurted out. "And the school is so big and confusing. I'll never fit in there, with all those people. And Dan Trapp is . . . he is horrible. I could stand everything else if he was helping my skating. But he's not! I'm getting worse, and they're going to make me try out now, and I'll just fail. They will end up kicking me out of Silver Blades. It will be awful!" Natalia hid her face in her hands. "I wish I could leave! But my father says I can't."

"Oh. Wow." Veronica sat down on the end of her bed and was quiet for a minute or two. "Look," she said finally, "you don't really have to stay here, do you? I mean, no one is holding a gun to your head. Why don't you just tell your dad you need to go home?"

Natalia blew her nose and pushed a lock of hair behind her ear. She shook her head sadly. "I tried," she said. "He won't let me. He thinks I just have to be patient, and everything will be okay. He doesn't understand at all."

Veronica crossed her legs under her and propped her head on her hand. "I guess it doesn't matter what country you're from," she said. "Parents are parents."

"Yes, Corinne and Roger are really strict with Tori," Natalia said.

"Sure. But I'd never let them run my life," Veronica told her. "You can't expect parents to understand anything. My mother sure doesn't. That's why I'm here, you know."

"I didn't know that," Natalia said.

Veronica shrugged. "Yeah. I got kicked out of a bunch of private schools in Europe. My mother was never around much, so I was pretty used to having my own way. But I like going to Kent Academy."

Veronica was a year ahead of Tori and Natalia in school. Her schedule was completely different from theirs, so Natalia rarely saw Veronica during school hours.

"I stay here because I like it," Veronica went on. "You know, Natalia, I bet you could find a way home if you wanted. If you really, really tried. I mean, it's important to do what you need to do," Veronica finished.

Natalia's eyes widened. "Are you serious?" she asked.

"Sure. You don't even have to tell your dad anything. If you want to go home, go home. Once you're there, what could he do about it?" Veronica asked.

"Nothing, I guess," Natalia said thoughtfully. "But, how could I do it? How could I ever get back to Russia on my own?"

Veronica laughed. "It's easy," she said. "You have to learn to be sneaky, like me. But it's worth it if you get what you want."

"I don't know," Natalia said. "I have never done anything like that before."

"You never got sent away from home before," Veronica pointed out.

"That's true," Natalia said. "And you think if I really need to go home, I'll be able to?" she asked.

"Absolutely," Veronica told her. "If you really want something, you'll find a way to get it."

Natalia sat up straighter on the bed. "I will do it," she decided. "Somehow, I will find a way to get back to Russia!"

9

"**H**ey, move over," Tori complained in a good-natured tone. "You guys are hogging all the room."

Natalia watched as Tori squeezed in next to Nikki, Patrick, and Alex on the couch.

"You know, you could sit on the floor," Alex teased. "Like Martina and Natalia. This couch is only so big . . ."

"No way," Tori said. "I put in my reservation for a seat on the couch. Just ask Haley. Besides, I'm really tired," she complained.

It was Saturday night, and the group was gathered at Haley's house to watch the "Stars on Ice" skating special, which was just about to begin. Natalia wished she could have stayed at Tori's. Being here just reminded her that she didn't belong. She wasn't even a real member of Silver Blades.

Natalia looked from Nikki to Tori to Martina, wondering if one of them had complained to Mrs. Bowen about the tryout. Or maybe it was Amber. Amber had stayed home tonight because she had an upset stomach.

Natalia had tried to stay home, too. The last thing she wanted was to spend an evening with this group of friends, feeling like an outsider again. But Corinne and Roger insisted that she go with Tori. Natalia gave in. She didn't want to cause trouble now, anyway. Not while she was trying to think of a way to go home.

Alex made a joke that Natalia didn't hear, and the others burst out laughing. Natalia glanced at each of them in turn. She might never know who had complained to Mrs. Bowen about her tryout, but she wouldn't be surprised if it was someone in this room right now.

Not one of these people is really my friend, she thought. Why wouldn't they complain about me?

"You're just lazy and you know it," Patrick told Tori, who was still trying to claim a seat on the couch. "First come, first served, I say. And since we got here first . . ."

"Aw, come on," Tori pleaded. She turned to Alex. "What about you, Alex? You're a gentleman. Look— I've got this humongous bruise right here." Tori pulled up her leggings and pointed to the side of her knee where a dark purple welt was swelling.

"Can you guys believe it? I fell on my double axel

today!" Tori said. "Sitting on the floor will hurt." She stuck out her lower lip in an exaggerated pout.

"Yeah, like the rest of us don't have bruises all over," Alex grumbled, but he stood up. "Okay, you win," he said. "I guess I'll see if Haley needs some help, anyway." He strode out of the room and disappeared into the kitchen.

Natalia glanced sharply at Tori. Did Tori mention the double axel on purpose? she wondered. Natalia had finally given up practicing it. What was the use? Dan hadn't even mentioned it in days, and she knew she'd never get it right on her own. Had Tori noticed that Natalia wasn't doing the jump anymore? Was she trying to rub it in?

Tori gazed happily at the TV, ignoring Natalia. A moment later Alex and Haley came back into the den. Haley carried a tray of drinks. Alex grasped a huge bowl of popcorn in one hand and a bunch of flowers in the other. He set the bowl of popcorn down on the table.

"What are those for?" Martina asked, nodding at the flowers.

"Just something beautiful for all you lovely ladies," Alex said in a teasing voice. He handed the flowers, one by one, to each of the girls.

"For my favorite partner," he said as he bowed and handed a rose to Nikki.

"For your only partner, you mean." Nikki laughed and took the flower. "Where did you get these, anyway?"

"I took them out of a vase in the kitchen," Alex said. "Haley's mom won't mind."

"She brought home a huge bouquet last night," Haley explained. "There's lots more where those came from."

"And here's one for my favorite date," Alex went on as he handed a flower to Haley. "And my favorite movie-star stand-in," he said, giving a flower to Martina. She had once been a skating double in a movie.

Alex paused in front of Natalia. She stared down at the floor, embarrassed. She hardly knew Alex. He probably felt as awkward as she did about giving her a flower. He probably didn't know what to do with the extra flowers he was holding.

"For my favorite Russian skater," Alex finally said.

Natalia glanced at him in surprise. "Thank you," she said, beginning to smile.

"No problem." Alex bent and handed two flowers to Natalia.

She took the roses, but her smile faded instantly. Two roses! she thought. Did he know what that meant?

The other girls had each gotten one flower. Natalia flushed. In Russia people only gave an even number of flowers at funerals. To someone who was dead.

She glanced up at Alex, but he had turned away, still smiling. It was silly, Natalia told herself. Alex didn't mean anything by it. He probably didn't even know the custom of the odd and even flowers. Or did he?

"Quiet, you guys," Haley ordered. "It's starting."

Alex took a seat on the floor next to Haley, and everyone quieted down to watch the skaters.

"Wow," Patrick said when the first commercial came on. "I can't believe Brigitte Laurent. I've never seen anybody else who can jump like that."

"She is pretty incredible," Martina agreed. "That height!"

"Yeah. Those back flips!" Alex said. "I'd love to be able to do just one of those."

Tori and Nikki nodded in agreement.

"But she doesn't skate that well!" Natalia blurted out.

The others stared at her as if they couldn't believe what they were hearing.

"You're kidding, right?" Alex asked.

"No," Natalia said. "Laurent is one skater I really dislike. She is so jerky on the ice, and her footwork is totally mechanical."

"But she's a fantastic jumper," Tori argued.

"I don't agree," Natalia said. "She is so obvious about going into a jump. She jerks her head over her shoulder like this." Natalia demonstrated. "And then just leaps into it. There is no flow."

"Yeah, but look at the height she gets in her triple jumps," Tori said. "She almost looks like she's flying."

"I'll bet she lands a quadruple one of these days," Alex said. "That would really be something."

"Not unless she learns to skate first," Natalia muttered.

Martina laughed. "Boy, Natalia, if that's not skating!"

Natalia flushed. She felt as if they were ganging up on her. But they had touched a nerve, admiring Laurent. It was as if all of Natalia's held-in feelings needed to come rushing out.

"Wait, I think I know what Natalia means," Nikki cut in. "I'd rather watch someone like Cassandra Wells. She doesn't have as much power in her jumps, but she has a wonderful line. So graceful! I love the way she moves."

"Exactly!" Natalia agreed, relieved that someone finally agreed with her. "Wells is a real classical skater. Everything she does is incredibly beautiful on the ice."

"Oh, Wells is boring," Haley objected. "I always feel like we've seen all her moves before. Her costumes, too. The great thing about Laurent is you never know what she's going to do next. And I love her costumes. They're so dramatic!"

"Dramatic?" Natalia said. "Are you serious? They're just weird. All that black, filmy stuff. Ugh."

"Ugh nothing," Haley said. "They're great. Like that one with the black mask that she throws onto the ice at the beginning of her program? It's cool."

"You like that costume?" Natalia asked, amazed.

"But it's so ugly. And the mask is very foolish. I think she just uses it to distract people from her skating. She probably thinks that if everyone is watching what she's doing with the mask, they won't look at her feet."

"No way," Haley said heatedly. "And the mask *isn't* foolish. It adds drama and . . . and . . . I don't know . . ."

"Pizzazz?" Patrick suggested.

"Yeah," Haley agreed. "That's it. Pizzazz."

"What is 'pizzazz'?" asked Natalia.

"You know. Excitement. Flair," Patrick explained.

"Excitement," Natalia said in disgust. "Stupidity is more like it."

"Stupidity!" Haley exclaimed. "Just because you don't like her doesn't mean . . ."

Patrick held up his hands before she could go any further. "Okay, okay, you two, break it up. Let's not get into a fist fight here," he teased.

"Yeah," Alex added. "Haley's mom gets really upset when people bleed on her carpet."

Everyone laughed. "Listen," Nikki said. "How about you two just agree to disagree on this one?"

"Good idea," Tori said. "Look at it this way—it makes perfect sense that you'd like different skaters. Haley likes things that are kind of wild and unusual."

"That's true," Martina put in. "And Natalia has

all that ballet training, so her tastes are bound to be much more classic."

"Yeah. The punk and the prima ballerina," Haley joked. "That's us."

Natalia flushed. The prima ballerina? So that was how Haley saw her!

The rest of the group probably saw her that way, too. Natalia realized she should never have argued with Haley in the first place. Now she had made things even worse.

Oh well, what did it matter, anyway? So what if all she ever did around here was argue or stick her foot in her mouth. Soon she wouldn't have to worry about what Haley thought. Or Alex or Patrick or any of the others. She wouldn't worry about Silver Blades at all. She was going home. The sooner the better.

10

Natalia pushed open the door to Veronica's room. It was ten-thirty at night, and she was exhausted. All she wanted to do was put on her pajamas, brush her teeth, and fall into bed. After her argument with Haley, the rest of the evening had been torture. She'd wanted to go home, but she couldn't ask to leave without making Tori go home, too. And Tori wanted to stay. Plus, she really didn't want to insult Haley by leaving early. She'd already insulted Haley enough!

Natalia flicked on the overhead light and then stood frozen in surprise. Her things were all gone! Her dresser drawers stood open—and empty. The books she'd left on the desk had disappeared, as well as her alarm clock and the picture of her family that she kept on the dresser. The closet door was open wide, but her clothes and her skating dresses were nowhere to be seen.

Where was everything?

"Oh, hi!" Veronica breezed into the room behind her. "I had a brainstorm," Veronica announced. "Since you're not going to be around much longer, I figured I might as well rearrange things in here for me. So I moved your stuff to Tori's room," she said.

"But, Veronica, I have no idea when I can leave," Natalia protested.

"Yes, but you're planning to go," Veronica said.

"I don't have any real plan—none at all!" Natalia exclaimed. "I thought you might help me, but . . ."

Veronica waved her protests aside. "Oh, a plan's no big deal. Something will work out, you'll see. It always does. Anyway, I figured you and Tori should really share a room, since you're on the same schedule. I can't stand hearing that alarm go off so early! I mean, it's still dark outside," Veronica said.

Natalia stared at her in disbelief. "Is everyone trying to get rid of me?" she asked.

"Oh, no!" Veronica said. "It's nothing personal. I mean, at first I thought it would be fun to be roommates. I like you, Natalia," Veronica went on. "But the hours you keep are too crazy for me. I need my sleep, you know."

"My hours!" Natalia's mouth dropped open. "I can't believe *you* are complaining about *my* hours!

After all the nights you woke me up in the last two weeks! I even covered for you when Corinne or Roger asked what time you came in!''

"And I appreciate that, I really do," Veronica assured her.

"But . . ." Before Natalia could say more, Tori stuck her head in the open doorway.

"Hey, what's going on?" she demanded. "How come Nat's stuff is all over my room?"

Veronica repeated her explanation.

Natalia couldn't believe this was happening. "This is silly," she tried to say. "I don't think I can—"

"Live with Tori?" Veronica finished for her. "Well, I know it will be difficult," she said with a grin. "I wouldn't want her for a roommate, either." She smiled teasingly at Tori. "But really, it can't be helped."

"That's not what I meant," Natalia replied, her voice rising. "I didn't mean anything about having Tori as a roommate. I meant that—"

"Cute, Veronica," Tori cut her off. "Really cute," Tori said, crossing her arms over her chest. "You know my room isn't big enough for two people. And how dare you even touch my things!" She glared at Veronica.

"What's the matter?" Veronica said. "I didn't touch anything personal. I've got better things to do. I just made a little room for Natalia's things."

"But my room is only half the size of yours!" Tori

protested. "There isn't enough room for two sets of things."

"Sure there is," Veronica said. "All you have to do is rearrange the furniture a little. And you already have an extra bed under the daybed," Veronica said. "You can just roll it back under your bed during the day."

"That's not fair!" Tori said. "This isn't your house. You can't just take over any way you want!"

"Really, Tori," Veronica scolded. "I can't believe you're making such a big deal out of this. It's rude. And juvenile. Besides," she lowered her voice, "think how Natalia will feel. As if you don't want her around."

Tori snapped her mouth shut. She looked at Natalia, and her face turned bright red.

Natalia felt just as embarrassed. It was awful to have Tori and Veronica arguing about who got stuck with her, as if she wasn't even there.

Tori was silent a moment. She finally said, "Come on, Nat. Let's go put your things away." She turned her back on Veronica.

"Wait," Veronica said. "I couldn't move the dresser by myself. Natalia will need it. You'll have to help me."

Natalia and Tori helped Veronica lift the heavy wooden dresser in Veronica's room. Together they managed to carry it down the hall to Tori's room.

"It doesn't even match my furniture," Tori grumbled as they set it down in a corner.

"Picky, picky, picky," Veronica said. "You'll make it look very nice with a vase and some pictures on top. See?" Veronica set the photo of Natalia's family on top of the dresser. Then she left the room.

Natalia stared at Tori, and Tori stared back at Natalia. "I guess we better rearrange the furniture," Tori said.

They worked silently for a while, shoving both beds against one wall and putting the desk between the windows.

"I hate to say it, but Veronica was right," Tori admitted. "It is possible to fit everything in."

"Well, the room is pretty crowded," Natalia said.

"Yeah. But I kind of like it," Tori said. She glanced at her watch. "I still have some reading to do for English, though. If I don't do it tonight, I don't know when I'll get it done." She sat down at her desk and turned on the light. "Sorry, Nat. I hope you weren't planning to go to bed right away," Tori added.

Natalia stifled a yawn. "No," she lied. She got out a book and looked around. The only place to sit was on the bed.

Natalia decided to give Tori her privacy. She wouldn't spend any more time in Tori's room than she absolutely had to.

"I'm going downstairs to get a snack," she said and left.

Downstairs in the kitchen, Natalia helped herself to a container of yogurt from the refrigerator. She had only snacked lightly at Haley's house. She sat at the table to eat. More than ever, she wished she could think of a way to go home.

"Hi!" It was Corinne. "Having a late snack?" she asked. She opened the refrigerator and pulled out a pitcher of iced tea.

"Yes." Natalia ate her yogurt slowly, taking teeny bites. Could she make it last until Tori was ready for bed?

Corinne picked up a stack of envelopes that was lying on the counter and started flipping through them. "I forgot to give this to you earlier." She handed an envelope to Natalia. "Mail for you."

"Really? Oh, thank you," Natalia said. She tore the envelope open and took out a letter. Three small pieces of paper fluttered into her lap. She quickly read the letter, which was handwritten in Russian:

My dearest Natalia,
Our company will be performing in Scranton, Pennsylvania, soon. I am told that this city is not far from Seneca Hills, where you are staying, so I am sending you three tickets to the ballet. We will be performing *Les Sylphides*, which I know you love. Unfortunately I will not have much time to visit after the performance, as we have a farewell party to attend that night. We will be leaving for home the next day. Still, it would give me great pleasure to see you again, however briefly. If you are able to come,

meet me outside the back door of the theater
after the performance. I'll be looking for you.

> With love and affection,
> Your cousin Viktor

Viktor! Natalia's eyes widened, and her heart began to pound furiously. That's it! She snatched up
the tickets and kissed them. These weren't just tickets to the ballet. These were her tickets home!

11

Natalia slipped off her black ballet slippers and tossed them into the bottom of her locker. She was glad class was over. Ms. Beaumont had fussed over her again today. Haley's comment about "the prima ballerina" had rung in her ears the whole time. Still, Natalia didn't feel too badly—because this was probably her last ballet class with the Silver Blades, anyway. Soon she'd be headed back home to Moscow. She couldn't wait to be in Russia again!

"Natalia?" Tori stood beside her, still wearing a pink leotard and white tights. Her ballet costumes were nowhere near as fancy as her skating dresses, Natalia noted with amusement. "I'm really having trouble with the form of that new leap we learned," Tori said. "I was wondering if you could help me?"

"I'm having a hard time with that, too." Martina joined them, looking at Natalia expectantly.

"Well, can you do it for me?" Natalia said.

Tori attempted the move, and then Martina. Natalia frowned. "Neither one of you is really extending your leg far enough," she told them. She placed her hands on Tori's leg and pulled gently. "See? You have to think of the hip as part of the leg," she corrected. "You need all the length you can get to give you that long, graceful line."

Haley looked up from her backpack, which she had emptied onto the bench she was sitting on. "I think Ms. Beaumont thinks you should just give up skating and become a ballerina instead," she said.

Natalia flushed slightly and stole a glance at Nikki, who was taking her skating clothes out of her locker. Nikki looked up, but Natalia couldn't tell if Haley's comment bothered her.

"How did you get so good at ballet, anyway, Natalia?" Haley asked as she sorted through her things.

"I have been taking ballet since I was four years old," Natalia explained. "Even longer than I have been skating. My mother loved to dance, and after she died, my father thought my sister and I should learn, too."

"Tori told us about how your mother died when you were really little," Haley said. She picked a Mickey Mouse Band-Aid out of her pile of stuff and placed it over a blister on her heel.

"That's terrible," Martina remarked. "Do you remember her at all?"

"Not really," Natalia replied. "My father says she loved ballet very much. Her sister, my aunt, loved it, too. It was something they both wanted to pass on to their children. My aunt's son dances with the Moscow Ballet," she said proudly. "My cousin Viktor."

"You're kidding!" Nikki exclaimed. "They're famous! Viktor must be an incredible dancer."

"He is," Natalia said, smiling to herself. A wonderful dancer, and a wonderful cousin—because he was going to take her home!

"Wait a minute," Nikki said. "I think I saw an ad for the Moscow Ballet in the paper. Aren't they going to be in Scranton sometime soon?"

"Next weekend," Natalia told her.

"Hey, we should go," Tori said. "That would be tons of fun."

"Yeah, and Ms. Beaumont always says that watching ballet is good for our skating," Haley added.

"As if!" Martina said as she pulled a pretty blue sweatshirt over her head. "We'd never get tickets. I'm sure they're sold out by now."

"I have tickets," Natalia blurted out.

"You do?" Tori asked.

Suddenly Tori, Haley, Nikki, and Martina were staring at her. Then they were all talking at once.

"Wait, wait, you guys," Tori said, holding up her

hands. "Hold on! How come you never told me about this?" Tori asked Natalia.

She and the others waited, looking at Natalia expectantly.

Oh, why did I say anything, Natalia wondered. She hadn't meant to. The words had just popped out, all on their own.

Natalia's brow furrowed. Had she just ruined her plan? She told Veronica about Viktor and the tickets, and Veronica had been really helpful. The two of them had carefully worked out all the details of Natalia's escape.

Veronica would tell Corinne that she and Natalia were going to Betsy's house for the day. Instead Natalia would leave Betsy's and take a cab to the bus station. From there she would catch a bus to Scranton. Veronica had even found out that Natalia could walk to the theater from the station in Scranton.

"What's the matter?" Tori asked. "Can we go to the ballet or not? Why do you look so worried about it?"

"Oh," Natalia said. "It's nothing. But, um . . . I have only three tickets. That is all Viktor sent me."

"Well," Martina said, "obviously one ticket is Tori's, since Natalia is living with her."

"Right." Tori's face fell. "And one of them will have to be for my mom. Which only leaves one ticket—for Natalia."

"Your mom?" Alarm bells went off in Natalia's head. She had just ruined her plan. Because if Corinne went along, Natalia would never manage to sneak off with Viktor!

"Well, somebody's got to drive us there," Tori pointed out. "Scranton is three hours away."

"Could we take a bus?" Natalia asked.

Haley snorted. "Yeah, right. As if Mrs. Carsen would let you go off on your own. Never in a million years."

"Wait a second," Tori said. "She might, for this. She's extra busy at work right now. I bet she'd let us go alone. Especially if I get Roger to say yes first. And I know he will." Tori grinned.

"Great! And then you'll have one extra ticket. So one of us could come, too," Haley said. "Cool."

"Yeah," Tori agreed. "The hard part will be deciding who gets to go."

Nikki bent down on one knee and folded her hands together, begging. "Choose me. Please, please, please! I adore the ballet!"

Haley gave Nikki a playful shove, sending her sprawling to the floor. "Hey!" Nikki said.

Haley ignored her. She stepped in front of Nikki. "Choose me!" She made a goofy face. "I'll keep you laughing all the way to Scranton!"

Natalia giggled.

"Ahem. Excuse me," Martina said, trying to sound dignified. "But would you really want to take one of these clowns to the ballet? Either one of them will embarrass you in front of your cousin." Haley socked her lightly on the arm, and Martina rolled her eyes. "Wouldn't you rather be seen with some-one worldly and sophisticated? Someone who knows how to act around a star? Like me, for instance?"

They were all giggling now. Natalia wondered briefly how it would feel to really be their friend, laughing this way. But she knew they were only treating her like this because they wanted something from her. A few days ago that thought would have hurt. But it was easy to laugh with them now. It didn't matter what they thought of her. It wasn't important, now that she was going home.

Natalia felt a wave of relief. Maybe her plan was safe, after all. Maybe this way would be even better. She was a little afraid of traveling alone, anyway. It would be good to have someone else along for the trip.

She laughed along with them, then threw up her hands and shrugged. "I can't choose just one of you," she said. "It is impossible."

"You have to choose," Tori told her. "What are you going to do?"

Natalia suddenly grinned. "I have an idea. Because you all love to compete so much, let's have a little contest. Whoever does the best triple flip goes to the ballet."

Everyone nodded in agreement. "Okay. That sounds fair," Haley said. "Especially since I do a great triple flip."

"Then it's settled," Tori said.

Natalia glanced at her watch. "If we hurry and change, we can do it before practice starts."

A few minutes later they were all on the ice. "Okay, Martina, you go first," Natalia said. Haley and Nikki had recruited Kathy Bart, their coach, to judge the "competition."

Martina skated around the rink, building up speed, then did a three-turn and bent her left knee. She planted her right toe pick in the ice and leaped into the air. She pulled her arms in tightly and rotated before landing neatly on her right, back outside edge.

"Nice and clean," Kathy commented as Martina skated over to them. Natalia smiled at her. She probably would have picked Martina to go with her. Martina had been pretty nice to her all along. Not like a real friend, but pleasant, in her own way.

Haley went next. She did the same movements as Martina, but managed to get a little more height in the jump. Nikki did her jump last. She started off well but leaned too far to the left on her landing, and briefly touched down with her left skate.

"I really blew that," Nikki said as she skated over to the group. "But I usually do a great triple flip!" She looked so disappointed that Natalia actually felt sorry for her.

"It happens," Kathy said cheerfully. "No one lands every jump, every time. This time around, I'd have to say that Haley is the winner."

"Yes!" Haley punched one fist high in the air.

"I guess I agree," Martina added. She sighed. "Oh, well! I'm sure you'll enjoy the ballet for me."

"You bet we will." Haley grinned and clapped Natalia on the back. "Won't we, Nat?"

Natalia forced herself to smile at Haley. But she cringed on the inside. She couldn't help thinking about the way Haley had made fun of her and Ms. Beaumont. And about their argument over Brigitte Laurent. What would a whole day with Haley be like?

Oh, well, she thought. It's just one day.

"All right, girls, let's get down to some serious skating now," Kathy said. "Dan is waiting for you, Natalia."

Natalia thanked Kathy and skated over to Dan.

"Hello, Natalia!" Dan greeted her with his usual wide smile. "How's the energy flowing today?"

"Fine." Natalia grinned. Pretty soon she'd be free of Dan and his crazy ideas. She couldn't wait to get back to Marina—to a real coach, and some real skating lessons.

"You look happy today," Dan said. "So let's see how that double axel looks now. I expect you've progressed quite a bit."

Natalia gaped at him in surprise. "My double axel?" she said. "It hasn't progressed at all!" How could it, when Dan hadn't been working with her on it? "But, I . . ." Natalia sputtered.

"Go on," Dan urged, "show me something terrific."

"I can't," Natalia protested.

"Sure you can," Dan said. "You can do anything you set your mind to. All the work you've been putting into that double axel is just going to come together. Let's see it."

Natalia frowned. "But I haven't been working on it," she told him. "I was waiting for you to show me what I am doing wrong," she explained.

Dan looked puzzled. "But we talked about that," he said. "You were going to work on building up some more speed. And on visualizing the jump. And on doing the exercises with the energy ball." He studied Natalia's face intently. "Didn't you do any of that?"

"No," Natalia said. "I did try to skate faster. But I didn't want to just practice the same old things. I did not believe you wanted me to work by myself. That's not how I did things in Russia."

Dan frowned. "It seems we've had a terrible misunderstanding here. Well, then, we'd better get to work. Let's see your double axel, anyway. Then we'll talk."

Natalia circled the rink, building up speed for the double axel. She took off—and completed only two rotations.

Talk, talk, talk, Natalia thought as she landed the disappointing jump. Dan could talk for a million years. He still couldn't help her. She had to get back to Russia—and fast!

12

"**B**us three fifty-seven to Pittsfield is now boarding. Bus three fifty-seven to Pittsfield." The loudspeaker crackled with static.

Natalia, Tori, and Haley stood in the run-down bus station in the center of town. They looked out of place, Natalia thought. They were all dressed up for the ballet. Even Haley had set aside her usual jeans, T-shirt, and hiking boots. Instead she wore a long black skirt, a little black top, and a pair of chunky shoes. A small silver hoop danced from one earlobe.

Tori wore a calf-length flowered dress with a lace collar. Natalia had on her soft-pink suit. Natalia had done her best to choose an outfit that would look good on the plane home, too. She wasn't able to bring a change of clothes. Only Veronica knew she would soon be leaving Seneca Hills for good.

Natalia was afraid Tori and Haley would get suspicious if she filled her black nylon backpack full of clothes. So it was mostly empty. At the last minute, though, she'd stuffed her skates into the bottom of the pack.

She just couldn't bear to part with her skates, not when they were so perfectly broken in. She had to be careful not to let on how heavy the pack was, though, or her secret would be out.

The loudspeaker crackled again. "Bus four-o-five to Scranton, now boarding. Bus four-o-five to Scranton."

"That is us?" Natalia asked. "Did he say Scranton?"

"You're right! That *is* us! Let's go!" Haley grabbed Natalia and Tori each by an arm and pushed them through the terminal.

Out in the parking lot several big blue-and-white buses waited. The strong smell of diesel fumes filled the lot.

Natalia boarded the bus, and Haley and Tori followed.

"Here are three seats together," Haley said as they pushed their way to the back. Haley slid into the window seat, and Tori sat next to her.

Natalia eased her heavy backpack off her shoulder, careful not to let it land with a clunk. She was just about to sit down when Haley suddenly grabbed her wrist and pulled.

"Wait!" Haley cried. "Don't sit down!"

"Why not?" Natalia looked at Haley, who pointed to the seat. Natalia glanced down and gasped. A sticky chocolate ice cream bar was melting into the upholstery.

"Ugh," Natalia said. "That's awful. Now what will I do? I can't sit here!"

Haley started to giggle. "Fooled you!" she said. She reached over and grasped the wooden stick. The melting "ice cream" came up with it, all in one piece.

Natalia stared. "Oh! It's fake."

Tori rolled her eyes. "Typical Haley joke," she said. "Don't mind her, Nat." She patted Haley on the head, and Haley made a face at her.

"Haley's got a weird sense of humor," Tori went on. "She can't resist playing jokes on people. I'm surprised she hasn't gotten you before."

Natalia took her seat. "I don't mind, really. I have a cousin who is always playing jokes on people, too," she said. "Her name is Maya—she is Viktor's little sister."

"Really?" Haley asked.

Natalia nodded. "There was one time, at dinner, when my grandmother asked her to pass a jug of water. So Maya did this . . ." Natalia made a face and groaned as if she were lifting something very heavy. "Finally she put the jug in front of my grandmother. Then my grandmother lifted the jug. She pulled it up really hard, because she expected it to be heavy. But it was almost empty. So the jug went flying up in the air, and water splashed all over the place." Natalia giggled, remembering the scene.

"Maya fell off her chair, she was laughing so hard." Natalia giggled harder.

Tori and Haley giggled, too. "That's a good one," Haley said. "I can't wait to try it on someone."

"It won't work on me, though," Tori said. "For once I'll know exactly what you're up to."

"I will have to tell Maya I passed her trick on to an American girl," Natalia said. "She will like that."

"Too bad I can't meet her," Haley said, grinning broadly. "I'd love to trade ideas with her."

Tori groaned. "No, please," she said. "You have enough ideas of your own. The last thing you need is encouragement!"

Tori started to laugh. "Remember the time at skating camp when you gave Carla Benson whipped cream with gravy and told her it was potatoes? Boy, Nat, you should have seen the look on her face when she tasted them!"

"Yeah, and you should have seen the look on your face when I showed up at your mom's wedding in my micro miniskirt!" Haley said.

"Haley and our friend Jill were bridesmaids when my mom married Roger," Tori explained. "It was a huge formal wedding."

"Yeah," Haley said. She leaned over Tori to make

it easier to talk to Natalia. "We were supposed to wear these beautiful, long dresses. But I happened to be wearing my combat boots during a fitting. Then I tripped and stepped on the dress and . . ." She made a loud ripping noise.

"Oh, no, Haley!" Natalia exclaimed. "You didn't!"

"I did," Haley said. "I tore the dress all across the back. It was ruined. So then Tori and her mom decided to shorten all the dresses. Which was really nice of them," Haley added. "I felt terrible about tearing the dress."

"But then," Tori broke in, "Haley comes waltzing in the day of the wedding with an incredibly short dress. She claimed she decided we should all wear microminis! I was furious!" Tori put her hands around Haley's neck and pretended to throttle her.

Haley stuck out her tongue and crossed her eyes, clowning along with her.

Natalia giggled. "I can imagine," she said. "So what happened?"

Tori grinned. "The hem was only taped up," she explained.

"Yeah, all I had to do was take off the tape, and it was fine," Haley added. "But I sure wish I had a picture of the look on Tori's face when I walked in."

Natalia laughed, and Tori and Haley joined in.

It was strange, Natalia thought. She felt happier and more relaxed than she had since leaving

Moscow. For the first time, it actually felt as if Tori and Haley were really laughing with her, not at her.

Too bad that didn't change anything, Natalia thought. Tori and Haley still weren't her real friends. And she still wanted to leave. She had to leave. Her skating couldn't get better as long as she was working with Dan. And there was no way she could face the humiliation of the tryout!

Tori's voice interrupted her thoughts. "Of course," she pointed out, "sometimes Haley's jokes do get her in trouble. One time Kathy practically threatened to kick her out of Silver Blades because she thought Haley wasn't serious about skating—all because she liked to play tricks on people."

"I accidentally brought a laugh box to practice," Haley explained. "And it went off while Tori was talking. Kathy just about went ballistic."

Natalia looked confused. " 'Ballistic'?"

Haley and Tori both laughed. Natalia flushed. They were laughing at her again!

"That means, she got *really* mad," Haley said. "But you know, if Dan was my coach instead of Kathy, he probably would have thanked me for making everybody laugh, and then get relaxed or something."

"It's true." Tori sighed and leaned her head back on her seat. "Dan makes me laugh," Tori said. "Him and his stupid energy balls!" She made a face.

"Yeah, and always telling us to get in touch with our feelings, and all that weird stuff." Haley chuckled.

"Actually, I guess he doesn't make me laugh," Tori admitted.

"Yeah, right," Haley said. "What you mean is, he makes you want to scream."

Tori giggled.

Natalia looked at Tori in amazement. "Really?" she said. "You don't like Dan?"

"Oh, it's not that I don't like him," Tori said. "He's really, really nice. And he really cares about his skaters. But . . ." she hesitated.

"But what?" Natalia urged.

"Well, you know. The way he wants us to find the 'inner skater' and stuff—it makes me crazy sometimes," Tori admitted.

"Oh, Tori, I cannot stand him," Natalia blurted out. "He hasn't helped me at all!"

"Really?" Tori exclaimed. "You've never said anything about that! You should have told me. He's really a good coach. It just takes a while to get used to him."

"Yeah," Haley agreed. "And Tori should know. She actually quit Silver Blades when she first got assigned to Dan. But then she changed her mind."

"It's true. I hated him at first," Tori said. "And he still frustrates me sometimes. But he's also taught me a lot. More than I ever thought he could."

"Wow," Natalia said. "I wish you told me that before."

Tori shrugged. "You never asked. I thought the two of you were getting along great. You never complained about him or anything."

It was true, Natalia realized. She hadn't said anything. She just assumed that Tori and everyone else thought Dan was wonderful. She frowned.

"If you don't like Dan, why haven't you found another coach?" Natalia asked.

"Well, Kathy's schedule was full back then, and after I got mad and quit, I realized how much I wanted to stay in Silver Blades. So I decided to give Dan a chance," Tori replied. "I'm glad I did, too. He's taught me some real important things. Like putting emotion into my skating, instead of just doing the moves."

"It's true," Haley said. "I can see a big difference in the way Tori skates now."

"Thank you," Tori said. She placed one hand in front of her waist and pretended to take a little bow. She closed her eyes and lifted one arm out to the side. "Feel the energy ball," she said in a dramatic tone of voice. "Feel it moving from your shoulder, down to your elbow, and plopping onto the floor!"

Haley and Natalia giggled.

Tori opened her eyes. "I don't know. Maybe it works, maybe it doesn't. Either way, that's Dan for you," she said.

"It sure is," Natalia agreed.

The bus rolled down the highway. Natalia was surprised at how quickly the time passed. It felt easy now, chatting with Tori and Haley. They were discussing their favorite TV shows when the driver tapped on his microphone to make an announcement.

"We'll be making a brief stop here," he said. "Passengers may go inside the terminal to use the rest rooms and buy snacks, but the bus will depart again in fifteen minutes. So watch your time, people!"

Haley stood up. "Come on, let's hit the bathroom. I drank about a gallon of juice this morning."

A few minutes later they were in the women's rest room. Natalia entered a stall and locked the door.

When she was ready to leave, though, she couldn't turn the lock. "Hey," she yelled. "Something is wrong. I can't get out." She pounded her fist against the door. "The lock is stuck."

She heard Haley giggling on the other side, and then Tori saying impatiently, "Ha-ley! Let her out."

"Oh, all right," Haley said.

"What did you do?" Natalia asked from inside the stall.

"Just a little paper clip in the lock," Haley said. She giggled again. "Sorry. I couldn't resist."

Natalia shook her head. "Very funny, Haley," she said. "Now let me out of here! This place is disgusting."

"No problem." She heard Haley fiddling with

something on the other side of the door. "There," she said. "You're free."

Natalia tried the lock again, but she still couldn't move it. "It's still stuck," she called out.

"But I took the paper clip out. Honest," Haley protested.

Natalia frowned and shook the door. "Come on, Haley. This is not funny anymore. Take it out for real."

"Let me see," Tori said. Natalia heard her shake the lock on the other side of the stall door. "Uh-oh," she said. "She's really not kidding this time, Nat. Are you sure you can't open the door? Try again."

Natalia did try, but it was no use. "I can't move it at all," she said, feeling a bit of panic. "How am I going to get out of here?"

13

"I'll go get someone," Tori said. "I'll find a custodian or something."

"You can't," Haley protested. "By the time he could do anything, the bus will be gone. You'll have to do something else. Climb under the door, Natalia."

"There's not enough room," Natalia told her.

"She's right," Tori agreed. "The door and the walls come down practically all the way to the floor. No one could fit through there. Boy, Haley, you really got us into a big mess this time," Tori said.

Natalia jiggled the lock one last time in desperation. It still wouldn't open. It was hopeless.

"Hey!" Natalia heard from above her. She looked up and saw Haley peering down from the top of the partition between the stalls.

"If you can't go under, you have to go over!" Haley said. "Come on," she urged Natalia. "Throw me your backpack. Then climb up on the toilet, like me, and I'll help you over."

"No, no, that's okay," Natalia said hastily. She hoisted her backpack onto one shoulder, trying not to let on how heavy it was. "I can carry it myself."

"What's the matter?" Haley grumbled good-naturedly. "You think I'm going to run off with your backpack and leave you locked in there or something?"

"No," Natalia answered.

"Really? Because, actually, that was the plan all along," Haley joked. "We've really been plotting for days, just to steal your lovely leather backpack. But I guess it won't work. So hurry up, or we'll miss the bus. We'll find another way to steal it later!"

Natalia took off her shoes and kicked them into Haley's stall. Then she hiked up her skirt and stepped onto the toilet seat. She grabbed the top of the partition with both hands and braced her weight against one foot. Then she heaved herself up.

"That's it!" Haley yelled. She grabbed Natalia's leg and pulled.

"Oww," Natalia said. "Be careful. I need that leg!"

Haley giggled. "Sorry. Just trying to help." She pulled again, not quite as hard. As Natalia swung her body over the top of the partition, her backpack came loose and slipped off her shoulder. It was headed directly for Haley's face.

Haley dodged the backpack, tumbled off the toilet seat, and crashed into the other side of the stall.

"Watch out," Haley called. "I need that face!"

"Sorry!" Natalia said. She dropped over the partition and her feet hit the floor. She lost her balance and crashed right into Haley.

"Oof," Haley said. "Watch out! I need . . ."

"That body," Natalia finished with her, and she and Haley cracked up.

Natalia brushed the front of her sweater with her hand and slid her shoes back on. "Hey," she said. "I managed to stay clean!"

"See? That wasn't so bad, was it?" Haley asked.

"No," Natalia said. "Actually, I think you got the worst of it. At least I'm in good shape for wall climbing."

"Don't you mean stall climbing?" Haley asked.

"Yeah," Tori said. "Hey, maybe it'll become the next new Olympic sport. You can be the first person to win a gold medal in it, Nat!" They all cracked up as Natalia and Haley burst out of the stall into the bathroom. Tori stood with her hands on her hips.

"Serves you right, Haley," Tori said. "Maybe next time you'll think twice before locking someone into a gross and disgusting place like this." She grabbed Natalia's arm. "Now, come on, the bus!"

They raced out of the bathroom. Natalia led them across the terminal as they ran through the station, dodging anyone who got in their way. But as they burst through the door to the parking lot, Natalia came to a sudden halt.

"Oh, no," she cried. "I don't believe it!"

The bus was gone.

Natalia felt a knot form in the pit of her stomach. "Now what are we going to do?" she cried.

Tori turned to Haley. "You and your stupid tricks!" She groaned. "I can't believe this!"

Haley's face turned pale. "I'm sorry," she said. "It was just a joke."

Natalia was speechless. She didn't care so much if they missed the ballet. But if she didn't get to Scranton in time to meet Viktor, how would she get home?

"Maybe there's another bus to Scranton," Haley said.

Natalia's spirits rose and she found her voice again. "Of course," she said. "After all, this is America! There is plenty of everything here—including buses!"

"We can't miss this ballet," Tori complained. "And my mother will kill us. I kept telling her how grown-up and responsible we'd be. She'll never let me forget this!"

"And she probably won't let you go anywhere alone for the rest of your life," Haley added.

"Well, don't just stand here," Natalia said. "Let's go!"

Natalia led the way across the lobby. She hurried up to the ticket desk and asked the woman behind the counter when the next bus to Scranton would leave.

"Four-thirty," the woman said.

Natalia's heart sank. "Five hours from now?"

Natalia turned to Haley and Tori, who were just catching up to her. "If we take the next bus, the ballet will be over when we get to Scranton," she said.

And that would be too late to find Viktor and tell him her plan, Natalia thought. And there was no other way she could get in touch with him. She didn't even know what hotel he was staying at!

Natalia wandered over to a bench and sat down heavily. She dropped her backpack on the floor, not even bothering to set it down gently. But neither Tori nor Haley noticed the way it clunked as it hit the ground.

Natalia felt like crying. It just couldn't be true. She wasn't going home! She was stuck in America, with Dan as her coach, facing total humiliation at the tryout.

Tori sat next to Natalia. "I wanted to go, too, but maybe we could go another time," she said.

"I feel terrible," Haley added. "But Tori's right. We'll go another time. I'll even pay for the tickets."

"It's not just the ballet," Natalia said. "It's . . . Viktor . . . I wanted . . ." She hesitated. She couldn't tell them the real reason she was upset.

There was a long silence. Finally Tori spoke. "I guess we'll just have to go back to Seneca Hills."

"No way," Haley declared. She rushed back to the ticket counter.

"What's she doing now?" Natalia asked.

Before Tori could reply, Haley raced up to them.

"It's okay," Haley said. "We can still get there! Come on." She reached for Natalia's pack, but Natalia grabbed it first. Haley gave her a puzzled look, then pulled Natalia toward the side door. Tori followed them.

An empty cab waited at the curb. Haley opened the back door and motioned them inside. "Come on, guys. Let's go to the ballet."

"We're taking a cab?" Natalia asked in amazement. "But will it cost a fortune?"

Haley grinned. "We won't go all the way to Scranton, turkey-brain. The lady told me that there's a train station on the other side of town. And there's a train leaving there for Scranton in half an hour."

"Hooray!" Tori cheered. "The cab's on me. I

brought extra money for souvenirs, but this is an emergency!"

Natalia didn't hesitate for a second. She climbed into the cab. A huge grin spread across her face. "To the train station, driver!"

"We're here—that is the Scranton Public Theater. I can't believe we made it!" Natalia pointed across the street as they pulled up to the curb. They had caught the train to Scranton and then taken another cab to the theater.

"Just stick with the girls of Silver Blades," Tori said. "We're true winners, in every way."

"Also very modest," Haley added, grinning. She looked at her watch. "The train was faster than the bus. We've got an hour until the ballet starts."

Natalia wouldn't have minded if they'd arrived an hour after the show started. As long as she was in time to meet Viktor, she was happy.

Tori paid the driver. The girls piled out of the cab and crossed the street. They had to push their way through a thick crowd of people on the steps of the old building. A tall, heavyset man accidentally bumped into Natalia. Her backpack slid off her shoulder and thumped onto the ground. Everything spilled out. Natalia dropped to her knees. Her heart was beating hard. But her skates were so heavy they hadn't spilled out.

Natalia gathered her other belongings together. She pulled the backpack hastily onto her shoulder again.

"Are you okay?" Haley asked.

"Fine," Natalia answered.

They joined the line of people waiting to enter the theater lobby. Natalia dug a hand into her backpack to get the tickets out of her wallet. Her wallet wasn't there.

The line drew closer to the theater. Natalia began to search more frantically. Hairbrush, passport, a small paperback book, the miniature screwdriver she used to tighten the blades on her skates, tissues, a mirror, lip gloss, mascara, and her skates. Everything except her wallet!

"I don't believe it," Natalia cried. "It's gone. My wallet is gone!"

"It can't be!" Tori exclaimed. "Let me look." She reached for the backpack, but Natalia quickly wrapped both arms around it and held it close to her chest. "It's not here. I'm sure."

"Okay, okay," Tori grumbled. "You act like I'm trying to steal something. What have you got in there, anyway, Nat?"

"Nothing," Natalia said. "Just some stuff. But what are we going to do?" she asked.

"You probably lost it when all your stuff fell out of your backpack," Tori said.

"No," Natalia insisted. "I put everything back in

my backpack, I'm sure. I checked all around the steps to make sure."

"Maybe it will turn up later," Tori said.

"In the meantime, we'll just explain you lost the tickets," Haley said. "And if they give us a hard time, Viktor can say who we are, right?"

"Right." Natalia felt a wave of relief. "How could they not let us in?"

The line moved forward and Natalia, Tori, and Haley stepped into the lobby. "Tickets, please." A chubby man in a dark jacket held out his hand.

"I'm sorry," Natalia said. "But I lost our tickets. My cousin is in the ballet, and he sent them to me. I had them in my wallet, and now I can't find it. I guess I dropped it somewhere."

The chubby man frowned. "Then I can't let you in. I'm sorry."

"But you have to," Tori said. "Didn't you hear her? Her cousin is one of the dancers."

The man laughed. "Sure he is. Nice try, girls. But no tickets, no seats." He reached around the girls to take tickets from a man and woman behind them. "Next, please," he said.

Natalia stepped back and noticed a phone on the wall. "Excuse me," she said to the man, "but could you please call backstage and get my cousin? His name is Viktor Petronsky."

The man stared at her as if she were out of her

mind. "I most certainly will not. Now, if you'll excuse me."

"Then we would like to speak to the manager, please," Natalia told him.

"And we won't leave until we do," Tori added.

The man glared at them. "Fine," he said. He reached for the phone and spoke quickly.

A few minutes later a tall silver-haired man approached the girls. "I understand you're trying to get into the ballet without tickets," he said.

"No, no," Natalia replied. "We had tickets. They were sent to me by my cousin. But I lost my wallet, and the tickets were inside."

The manager raised his eyebrows. "A group of girls tried the same trick last week. Friends of yours, I suppose," he said. "It won't work this time. I'm surprised you'd even try."

"But we don't know those girls," Natalia explained. "I am telling the truth. All we need is to call my cousin backstage. He will tell you. Please—just let me talk to Viktor."

"That isn't allowed." The manager grasped Natalia by the elbow. "Come along," he said. "The game is over."

Natalia felt a burst of helpless panic. "But I told you, I don't know those other girls," she said. "We went through so much trouble to get here! I don't even care about the tickets anymore. Just call Viktor! Please!"

Natalia was desperate. The manager had to believe her. He had to let her see Viktor, or else her plan would be ruined. This was her last chance.

"Sorry. I told you I'm not playing this time," the manager repeated. "I'll give you one last chance to leave quietly. If you don't, I'll call the police. Immediately."

15

"**I**'m sure the Russian ambassador to the United States wouldn't like that," Tori said. Her voice was so loud that people in the lobby stopped and stared.

Natalia felt a wave of dismay as a small crowd began to gather around them.

Tori gestured to Natalia. "This happens to be the ambassador's daughter, Natalia Cherkas," she said. "Natalia, maybe you should call your dad. I'm sure he'd love to hear that this man won't let you see your own cousin."

Natalia hesitated. Tori poked her in the side. Natalia realized she had to play along with Tori if she had any hopes of getting in to see Viktor.

"Um, I think you are right," Natalia said. She

scanned the lobby. "There must be a pay phone here somewhere."

The manager glanced at the crowd of people who were watching them. He ran a hand through his hair and sighed.

"All right, I'll call Mr. Petronsky for you. But if this is a prank, I *will* call the police," he warned.

"Thank you," Natalia said.

The manager disappeared.

Tori grinned at Natalia. "See? I told you the girls of Silver Blades are winners!" She threw an arm around Natalia's shoulder. "Don't worry, Nat!"

Natalia felt tears rush to her eyes. She couldn't help it. It was all too much. Her plan might be ruined for good, and here was Tori, calling her that awful name!

"Don't call me 'Nat'!" Natalia exploded. She shook Tori's arm off her shoulder. "I hate that stupid name."

Tori blinked in astonishment. "Sorry," she said. "It's just a nickname. I thought it was cute."

"We didn't know it bothered you," Haley added.

"Well, it does!" Natalia cried. "It bothers me a lot. Just like all the other nasty things you do to me."

"What nasty things?" Tori stared at Natalia in disbelief. "Tell me what you're talking about!"

"Not in front of all these people!" Natalia pulled Tori out of the middle of the lobby into a corner.

"Boy, you really care about your privacy," Haley said.

"Of course I care! I hate to have people staring at me, making me feel like an idiot," Natalia declared.

"Really? Oh." Tori shrugged. "Sorry for being so clueless," Tori said.

"Huh? Being what?" Natalia asked in confusion.

Tori and Haley burst out laughing—as usual. Natalia flushed red with embarrassment. She wanted to tell them exactly how awful they made her feel. But at that moment, a loud voice rang out across the lobby.

"Natalia, wait!" someone called in Russian.

Natalia turned. A tall, muscular young man raced through the lobby. A long robe covered his ballet clothes. The heavy stage makeup he wore didn't hide the scowl on his handsome face.

"Viktor!" Natalia cried. She took a few steps toward her cousin. It was so good to see his face!

"Natalia!" Viktor scooped her into a hug. "What's going on? Are you all right?" His deep brown eyes were full of worry as he looked closely at her.

"I am not all right," Natalia said. "I lost my wallet, and the manager wouldn't let me call you." From the corner of her eye, Natalia noticed that Haley and Tori couldn't take their eyes off Viktor. They looked totally starstruck.

Natalia's manners took over. "Viktor, I want you to meet Tori and Haley," she said politely.

"Nice to meet you," Viktor told them, shaking their hands.

"I have to talk to you about something private," Natalia told Viktor in a low voice.

"All right," Viktor said, "but the ballet starts in fifteen minutes. I should not even be out here." People were slowing down as they walked past, eyeing Viktor with curiosity.

"I know," Natalia said. She asked Tori and Haley if she could have a few minutes to talk with Viktor alone. They agreed, and Natalia walked to the other side of the lobby with Viktor. She shrugged off her heavy backpack and set it on the floor.

"I want to go home," Natalia blurted out in Russian. "I want you to take me to Moscow with you. Tomorrow."

Viktor frowned. "What are you talking about? I thought you were going to spend the year in America."

"I was," Natalia said. "But I don't like it here. I want to leave." She shifted from one foot to the other nervously.

"What about your father? Does he know about this?" Viktor asked.

"Yes! I told him I was unhappy," Natalia said.

Viktor put his finger under her chin and tipped her head up so that she had to meet his eyes. "And what did he say?"

Natalia hadn't expected Viktor to be so difficult.

"He says I should stay here. That I have to have patience. But he doesn't understand how bad it is," she explained.

"And how bad is it?" he asked. "What is so terrible?"

"Everything is terrible," she said, bursting into tears. "The other kids make fun of me. They laugh at the things I say. I'll never have any friends here."

Viktor hugged her again. "It can't be so bad. What about your skating?" he asked.

"Awful!" Natalia exclaimed. "I'm getting worse, not better. I want to go back to Marina."

Viktor wiped the tears off Natalia's cheeks. "I see," he said thoughtfully. "You've worked with just one coach all your life, haven't you?" Viktor asked.

"Almost," Natalia conceded. "I've been with Marina since I was eight."

"And how long have you been in America now?"

Natalia sighed. "Three weeks. The worst three weeks of my life."

Viktor laughed and shook his head. "Three weeks is not much time to get to know someone. I don't think you've given this coach a fair chance yet. He has a good reputation, doesn't he?"

"Yes, but . . ." Natalia began.

"And wasn't he quite successful as a skater himself?"

Natalia nodded. "He placed at the Worlds, I think. But that was so long ago!"

"Still, he must know something about skating," Viktor insisted.

"But what good is that if I don't understand him?" Natalia protested.

"Have you told him that?"

"No," Natalia admitted.

"Then maybe you need to," Viktor said gently. "How else is he going to know?"

"I don't know," Natalia said. "I don't even want to tell him. I just want to go home and have everything be the way it used to. I'm tired of being laughed at!"

"When you're in a foreign country, you're bound to make mistakes," Viktor told her. "You have to learn to laugh things off sometimes."

"You sound just like my father," Natalia grumbled.

"Then perhaps we are both right," Viktor said. "Imagine if you put these girls in Moscow. Wouldn't they make a few mistakes? And wouldn't you laugh at them?"

"No," Natalia insisted. "Anyway, they don't like me, I can tell." Even as she spoke, though, doubt crept in. They'd gone to a lot of trouble to make sure she saw Viktor.

"They don't like you?" Viktor asked, smiling affectionately. "Natalia, how could anyone not like you? I don't believe that."

"But they don't." Natalia pushed her doubts aside. She wanted to go home, and that was that. "They just don't," she insisted.

"Of course they do," Viktor said. "I'm sure of it. So sure, in fact, that I'll prove it to you." He took her hand and pulled her across the lobby to Tori and Haley.

"Girls," he said, "I'm taking Natalia home with me tomorrow."

16

Natalia stared at Viktor in astonishment. "Do you mean it?" she asked him eagerly.

"Of course," Viktor answered.

"But why?" Tori asked. "She just got here!" She looked suddenly concerned. "Did something happen to your grandmother? Or your sister?"

"Oh, no," Viktor said. "It's nothing like that. Everything is fine at home."

"But if everything is okay . . . I don't understand," Haley said.

"I won't let Natalia stay here," Viktor said firmly. "It is not good for her to live with people who do not like her."

"Wait a minute!" Tori turned to Natalia. "You told him we don't like you? But that's not true at all!"

"Of course we like Natalia," Haley told Viktor. "We like her a lot. Everybody does."

Natalia stared at them, astonished. "But—but, you are always laughing at me! Like, when I don't understand something you say," she burst out. "Like before, when you used the word 'clueless.' It was so mean, the way you laughed at me."

"I'm sorry," Haley said. "We didn't mean to be nasty. You just looked so puzzled. 'Clueless' just means you don't understand something."

"Well, I know what *that* feels like," Natalia said. "But that doesn't mean you have to laugh at me. I am not trying to be funny, you know."

"We really are sorry," Tori told her.

"Well, there are other things that are worse," Natalia said. Now that she had started complaining, she couldn't seem to stop. "I don't like feeling that I'm in your way all the time," she said to Tori. "I know you don't like sharing a room with me."

Tori started to say something, but Natalia rushed on. "And I don't understand Veronica at all," she said. "First she acted like she wanted to be friends, and then she kicked me out of her room. Why did she do that?"

"That's easy," Tori said. "Because she's selfish and bossy. Veronica thinks she can do whatever she wants, whenever she wants." Tori leaned against the wall and crossed her arms. "At first she wanted a roommate, and then she didn't. Who knows why? Believe me," Tori continued, "I don't understand her, either. But I do know one thing: Whatever she did, it had nothing to do with you. Maybe it was a way to make me really mad. We don't exactly get along, you know."

"Oh," Natalia said. She was quiet for a moment. It hadn't occurred to her that Veronica's actions weren't directed at her.

"Well, I hated being deserted in school when I didn't know my way around," Natalia went on. "And I hated being made fun of because I'm good in ballet. And—"

"Wait! Wow," Haley said. "I can't believe you've been feeling like this all this time and never said a word." She shrugged helplessly. "I'm really sorry. I wasn't making fun of you," she explained. "I was just trying to make people laugh, as usual. If anything, I was teasing Nikki for being jealous."

"You have to know Haley to understand that she gets carried away sometimes," Tori said.

"But I don't know her. Not well," Natalia said.

Haley turned red. She glanced toward the front of the theater. Natalia looked in the same direction and saw the heavyset man who had knocked into her on the steps.

Haley turned to Natalia. "Listen, I just thought of something," she said. "I need to go check it out."

"Of course," Natalia told her. Obviously Haley was embarrassed and needed to get away.

"Really, Nat. I mean, Natalia. I wish you'd said something before now," Tori told her. "We really didn't know how you felt. There's one thing about being in Silver Blades that's totally special. We compete with each other and fight sometimes, but we're a team, too. On the ice and off."

"But I am not even in Silver Blades," Natalia said. "I haven't had a real tryout yet." And I never will, she added silently.

"So what?" Tori said. "You're in. You've been in ever since Dan saw your tape."

"This is what I thought, too," Natalia said. "But then Mrs. Bowen said I had to have an official tryout because someone complained. I think it might have been Nikki, because she was jealous of the way Ms. Beaumont treats me."

Tori shook her head. "No way," she said. "Nikki would never do that. It couldn't have been Nikki, or Haley, or Martina, or Amber, I'm positive. None of them would do something like that. And I sure didn't do it. It was probably someone who barely made it into Silver Blades. Anyway, all you have to do is skate. That's what Amber did. Her tryout wasn't 'official,' either. She just skated a new routine for Kathy and then she was in. It's no big deal," Tori finished.

"But that is a big deal," Natalia said. She looked down at her shoes and spoke so quietly Tori had to lean close to hear her. "I can't skate well enough right now. I can't even land my double axel. They will never let me in."

Tori was silent for so long that Natalia finally

looked up, wondering what was going on. Tori was staring at her with her mouth open and a look of absolute astonishment on her face. "You're not serious!" she said at last.

"Of course I am," Natalia said miserably.

"But Natalia," Tori said, "the tryout is only a formality for you. You could spend half the time on your rear end and you'd still make it. And lots of kids can't land a double axel. You're not the only one. But you can land plenty of other jumps."

"No," Natalia said. "I don't believe you. It can't be as easy as you say."

"It is," Tori insisted. "They're just afraid that if they break the rules for you, other people will expect to get in without a tryout. But everybody—I mean everybody—knows you skate well enough to be in Silver Blades." She paused. "Maybe you've been having a rough time lately, but who wouldn't? You moved far from home to a strange country, you're living with a new family, and you have a new coach! But anyone can see you have what it takes to be a great skater."

"Really?" Natalia asked. Her head was spinning. Everything Tori said was completely different from what she'd believed. She couldn't quite take it all in.

"Really," Tori said firmly. Before she could continue, Haley ran up with a brown wallet in her hand.

"Look at this," Haley said. "I found it! I saw that guy who bumped into you and remembered that I thought I saw him kick something across the steps. Whatever it was went flying into the bushes. I didn't pay much attention at the time. But it just occurred to me that it might be your wallet! It fell out of your backpack when he crashed into you, and that's what he kicked away!"

"That's great," Tori said. "Good work, Haley."

Natalia opened the wallet and took out the tickets. "Uh, yeah, thanks, Haley." She still couldn't think straight.

"You see?" Viktor asked. "Only your friends do such things to help you." He smiled at Natalia, and then at Tori and Haley. "And now, I have a ballet to perform."

"But Viktor . . ." Natalia protested.

"You girls talk," Viktor said. "And you think about this some more, Natalia. We will talk again after the show." He kissed her on both cheeks and hurried away.

Natalia was silent for a moment. So were Tori and Haley. Finally Tori spoke.

"You know, Natalia, maybe you should give up skating and become an actress," Tori said. "We really thought you were happy here. You had everybody fooled."

"I feel just terrible that you've been so unhappy, and we never even knew it," Haley added.

"Me too," Tori said.

Natalia suddenly smiled. "Everything seems so different now. How I feel about Dan, the tryouts,

even you two. I guess I've been really . . . clueless.
Even more than I thought I was!" she said, and they
all laughed together.

"You'll stay, then?" Tori asked. She and Haley
waited.

"Of course," Natalia told her. She had made her
decision without even realizing it. "So, come on,"
Natalia said. "It's time for the ballet."

Tori reached down and picked up Natalia's
backpack. "Wow," Tori said. "What have you got in
here, anyway?"

Natalia opened the drawstring at the top and
reached in. She pulled out her skates. "To take
home to Moscow. I couldn't bear to go without
them," Natalia explained.

Tori put an arm around Natalia's shoulder.
"Well," she said, "if there was any doubt before, this
really proves it."

"Proves what?" Natalia asked.

Tori grinned. "You are definitely one of us!"

17

atalia and Tori stood side by side in the basement. They stared at the huge pile of cardboard boxes they'd carried down from the study and stacked in a corner.

"That's it," Tori said. "The last two boxes. I can't believe it. I didn't think we'd ever finish."

"I know," Natalia agreed. "There must be fifty of them. What's in all these, anyway?"

"Who knows? Roger's junk. Probably his papers from college and his high-school yearbook and stuff like that," Tori said. "He said it doesn't matter what we do with them, as long as we don't throw them away."

Natalia put her hands on her hips and stretched, arching her back. "I'm glad he doesn't mind," she said, "because it will be really nice to have my own room."

"I don't know why I never thought of this in the first place," Tori said.

"I'm just glad you did," Natalia said.

A week had passed since Natalia had decided to stay in America. Tori and the other girls in Silver Blades had gone out of their way to be nice to her, and Natalia finally felt that they were all going to be good friends.

The only trouble was, Natalia knew Tori was not very happy about sharing her room. Then Tori had her brainstorm: Why not turn the downstairs study into a bedroom for Natalia?

Corinne and Roger agreed, and Natalia and Tori had cleared it out. Then Roger helped them move the roll-away bed and dresser from Tori's room downstairs. The study already contained a big oak desk and a beige upholstered chair. After they had rearranged the furniture, the room was cozy and inviting.

"Now comes the fun part," Tori said as she and Natalia hurried back upstairs. "Making your new room look really nice."

Natalia led the way into her new bedroom. Tori lifted a favorite watercolor of Roger's off the wall. "I think we can store this someplace else for now," she said. "I found some great posters in my closet. I thought you might like to put them up instead."

Natalia unrolled one of the posters that lay curled up on the floor. She gasped in delight. "It's Klimova and Naumov, the Russian pairs skaters! Thank you, Tori," she said. "This is great." She unrolled another poster. "Oksana Baiul!" Natalia exclaimed. "I love her!"

"These posters used to be on my wall, until I put up my new ones of Michelle Kwan," Tori said. "I thought they'd make you feel more at home," she said.

Natalia pinned the posters to the wall. "Thank you," she told Tori again. "Although I really haven't been homesick lately. Not since last weekend, and since I made it through the tryout!"

"I told you that was just a formality," Tori said. "Though, you skated so well, you would have been in even if you competed against a hundred skaters."

Natalia flushed with pleasure. She sat down in the big upholstered chair and drew her feet up under her. "It's funny, but I wasn't nervous at all," she said. "Not even a little bit. I thought I would be when I saw how many members of Silver Blades came to watch."

"I know." Tori sat on the bed near her. "Everyone wanted to cheer you on, to make sure you felt welcome. Most of the kids felt bad that you had to try out because somebody complained."

"Well," Natalia said, "it was only fair, I guess."

Veronica walked in, carrying a CD player. "I don't use this much anymore," she said to Natalia. "Not since I got a new one for my birthday. I thought maybe you'd like it."

"Great! Thank you," Natalia said.

"No problem." Veronica glanced around the room. "It's starting to look nice in here," she said. Veronica leaned closer to Natalia.

"Listen, since you're sticking around for a while, maybe you'll get to meet some of my friends after all," Veronica said. "Some night, you know?" She smiled secretively.

Natalia smiled back. "Maybe," she said. She didn't know if she'd go, but it was nice to be invited.

"Great," Veronica said. "See you guys later. Roger's giving me a ride to the library. I've got a paper to work on."

Veronica left, and Tori and Natalia exchanged grins. "Sure," Natalia said. "A paper!"

Natalia leaned back in the chair and gazed up at the posters of the Russian skaters. "I wonder if they have ever worked with energy balls," she said.

"Or tried to get in touch with their inner skaters." Tori giggled.

"You know, Dan is really trying hard to make sure I understand him," Natalia said. "And I landed my double axel twice yesterday!"

"That's great," Tori told her. "You see, America isn't such a bad place after all."

"No," Natalia agreed. "And you know what?" she asked Tori.

"What?" Tori asked back.

Natalia grinned. "I think I'm going to enjoy being an American!"

5: The Perfect Pair

Nikki Simon and Alex Beekman are the perfect pair on the ice. But off the ice there's a big problem. Suddenly Alex is sending Nikki gifts and asking her out on dates. Nikki wants to be Alex's partner in pairs but not his girlfriend. Will she lose Alex when she tells him? Can Nikki's friends in Silver Blades find a way to save her friendship with Alex *and* her skating career?

6: Skating Camp

Summer's here and Jill can't wait to join her best friends from Silver Blades at skating camp. It's going to be just like old times. But things have changed since Jill left Silver Blades to train at a famous ice academy. Tori and Danielle are spending all their time with another skater, Haley Arthur, and Nikki has a big secret that she won't share with anyone. Has Jill lost her best friends forever?

7: The Ice Princess

Tori's favorite skating superstar, Elyse Taylor, is in town, and she's staying with Tori! When Elyse promises to teach Tori her famous spin, Tori's sure they'll become the best of friends. But Elyse isn't the sweet champion everyone thinks she is. And she's going to make problems for Tori!

8: Rumors at the Rink

Haley can't believe it—Kathy Bart, her favorite coach in the whole world, is quitting Silver Blades! Haley's sure it's all her fault. Why didn't she listen when everyone told her to stop playing practical jokes on Kathy? With Kathy gone, Haley knows she'll never win the next big competition. She has to make Kathy change her mind—no matter what. But will Haley's secret plan work?

9: Spring Break

Jill is home from the Ice Academy, and everyone is treating her like a star. And she loves it! It's like a dream come true—especially when she meets cute, fifteen-year-old Ryan McKensey. He's so fun and cool—and he happens to be her number-one fan! The only problem is that he doesn't understand what it takes to be a professional athlete. Jill doesn't want to ruin her chances with such a great guy. But will dating Ryan destroy her future as an Olympic skater?

10: Center Ice

It's gold medal time for Tori—she just knows it! The next big competition is coming up, and Tori has a winning routine. Now all she needs is that fabulous skating dress her mother promised her! But Mrs. Carsen doesn't seem to be interested in Tori's skating anymore—not since she started dating a new man in town. When Mrs. Carsen tells Tori she's not going to the competition, Tori decides enough is enough! She has a plan that will change everything—forever!

11: A Surprise Twist

Danielle's on top of the world! All her hard work at the rink has paid off. She's good. Very good. And Dani's new English teacher, Ms. Howard, says she has a real flair for writing—she might even be the best writer in her class. Trouble is, there's a big skating competition coming up—*and* a writing contest. Dani's stumped. Her friends and family are counting on her to skate her best. But Ms. Howard is counting on her to write a winning story. How can Dani choose between skating and her new passion?

12: The Winning Spirit

A group of Special Olympics skaters is on the way to Seneca Hills! The skaters are going to pair up with the Silver Blades members in a mini-competition. Everyone in Silver Blades thinks Nikki Simon is really lucky—her Special Olympics partner is Carrie, a girl with Down syndrome who's one of the best visiting skaters. But Nikki can't seem to warm up to the idea of skating with Carrie. In fact, she seems to be hiding something . . . but what?

13: The Big Audition

Holiday excitement is in the air! Jill Wong, one of Silver Blades' best skaters, is certain she will win the leading role of Clara in the *Nutcracker on Ice* spectacular. Until young skater Amber Armstrong comes along. At first Jill can't believe that Amber is serious competition. But she had better believe it—and fast! Because she's about to find herself completely out of the spotlight.

14: Nutcracker on Ice

Nothing is going Jill Wong's way. She hates her role in the *Nutcracker on Ice* spectacular. And she's hardly on the ice long enough to be noticed! To top it all off, the Ice Academy coaches seem awfully impressed with Jill's main rival, Amber Armstrong. Jill has worked so hard to return to the Academy, and now she might lose her chance. Does Jill have what it takes to save her lifelong dream?

Super Edition 1: Rinkside Romance

Tori, Haley, Nikki, and Amber are at the Junior Nationals, where a figure skater's dreams can really come true! But Amber's trying too hard, and her skating is awful. Tori's in trouble with an important judge. Nikki and Alex are fighting so much they might not make it into the competition. And someone is sending them all mysterious love notes! Are their skating dreams about to turn into nightmares?

15: A New Move

Haley's got a big problem. Lately her parents have been fighting more than ever. And now her dad is moving out—and going to live in Canada! Haley just doesn't see how she can live without him. Especially since the only thing her mom and sister ever talk about is her sister's riding. They don't care about Haley's skating at all! There's one clever move that could solve all Haley's problems. Does she have the nerve to go through with it?

16: Ice Magic

Martina Nemo has always dreamed of skating in the Ice Capades. So when she lands a skating role in a television movie, it seems too good to be true! Martina loves to perform in front of the camera. It's a lot of fun—especially when all her friends in Silver Blades visit her on the set to cheer her on. Then Martina discovers something terrible: Someone is out to ruin her chance of a lifetime. . . .

17: A Leap Ahead

Amber Armstrong is only eleven, but she can already skate as well as—even better than—the older girls in Silver Blades. The only problem is that the other skaters still treat her like a baby. So Amber decides to take the senior-level skating test. She'll be the youngest skater ever to pass, and then the other girls will *have* to stop treating her like a little kid. Amber is sure her plan will work. But is she headed for success or for total disaster?

18: More Than Friends

Nikki's furious. Her skating partner, Alex, and her good friend, Haley, are dating each other. Nikki knows she shouldn't be jealous, but she is. She'd do anything to break them up. And she knows how to do it, too. But should she? Or will Nikki end up with no friends at all?

Super Edition 2: Wedding Secrets

It's happening! Tori's mom is getting married! Everything has to be perfect—the invitations, the bridesmaids' dresses, and especially Tori's big wedding surprise. No problem! Tori has it all under control. Until she gets a surprise of her own—a new stepsister, Veronica! Suddenly Veronica starts giving orders, and everyone's listening to *her*. Tori is steaming mad. But she knows Veronica is hiding something big. And Tori's going to find out what it is—before Veronica takes over the wedding, and the rest of Tori's life!

DO YOU HAVE A YOUNGER BROTHER OR SISTER?

Maybe he or she would like to meet Jill Wong's little sister Randi and her friends in the exciting new series

SILVER BLADES®

FIGURE EIGHTS

Look for these titles at your bookstore or library:

ICE DREAMS
STAR FOR A DAY
THE BEST ICE SHOW EVER!
BOSSY ANNA
DOUBLE BIRTHDAY TROUBLE
SPECIAL DELIVERY MESS
RANDI'S MISSING SKATES

LEARN TO SKATE!

SKATE WITH U.S.
A SPECIAL PROGRAM FOR BEGINNERS

WHAT IS **SKATE WITH U.S.?**

Designed by the United States Figure Skating Association (USFSA) and sponsored by the United States Postal Service, Skate With U.S. is a beginning ice-skating program that is fun, challenging, and rewarding. Skaters of all ages are welcome!

HOW DO I JOIN **SKATE WITH U.S.?**

Skate With U.S. is offered at many rinks and clubs across the country. Contact your local rink or club to see if it offers the USFSA Basic Skills program. Or **call 1-800-269-0166** for more information about the Skate With U.S. program in your area.

WHAT DO I GET WHEN I JOIN **SKATE WITH U.S.?**

When you join Skate With U.S. through a club or a rink, you will be registered as an official USFSA Basic Skills Member, and you will receive:

- Official Basic Skills Membership Card
- Basic Skills Record Book with stickers
- Official Basic Skills member patch
- Year patch, denoting membership year
  And much, much more!

PLUS you may be eligible to participate in a "Compete With U.S." competition hosted by sponsoring clubs and rinks!

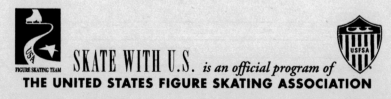

SKATE WITH U.S. *is an official program of*
THE UNITED STATES FIGURE SKATING ASSOCIATION

A FAN CLUB—JUST FOR YOU!

JOIN THE USA FIGURE SKATING INSIDE TICKET FAN CLUB!

As a member of this special skating fan club, you get:

- **Six issues of SKATING MAGAZINE!**
  For the inside edge on what's happening on and off the ice!

- **Your very own copy of MAGIC MEMORIES ON ICE!**
  A 90-minute video produced by ABC Sports featuring the world's greatest skaters!

- **An Official USA FIGURE SKATING TEAM Pin!**
  Available only to Inside Ticket Fan Club members!

- **A limited-edition photo of the U.S. World Figure Skating Team!**
  Available only to Inside Ticket Fan Club members!

- **The Official USA FIGURE SKATING INSIDE TICKET Membership Card!** For special discounts on USA Figure Skating collectibles and memorabilia!

To join the USA FIGURE SKATING INSIDE TICKET Fan Club, fill out the form below and send it with $24.95, plus $3.95 for shipping and handling (U.S. funds only, please!), to:

> Sports Fan Network
> USA Figure Skating Inside Ticket
> P.O. Box 581
> Portland, Oregon 97207-0581

Or call the Sports Fan Network membership hotline at **1-800-363-8796!**

NAME:_____

ADDRESS:_____

CITY:_____**STATE:**_____**ZIP:**_____

PHONE: (___)_____**DATE OF BIRTH:**_____